Sarah's Siblings
Book 9 in Clover Creek Caravan
Kirsten Osbourne

Copyright © 2022 by Kirsten Osbourne

Unlimited Dreams Publishing

All rights reserved.

Cover design by Erin Dameron Hill/ EDH Graphics

No part of this book may be reproduced in any form or by any electronic or mechanical means including information storage and retrieval systems, without permission in writing from the author. The only exception is by a reviewer, who may quote short excerpts in a review.

This book is a work of fiction. Names, characters, places, and incidents either are products of the author's imagination or are used fictitiously. Any resemblance to actual persons, living or dead, events, or locales is entirely coincidental.

Kirsten Osbourne

Visit my website at www.kirstenandmorganna.com

Dedication:

I never remember to dedicate my books. It's not that there aren't people around me who deserve it, I simply forget. This time, though, I remember. This book is dedicated to my father-in-law, the best man I've ever known, who is dying a few feet from me as I type this. My family and I came to Texas (from Idaho) in May to help out with him as we knew he wasn't long for this world.

Now he is on hospice, and I've been sitting up with him all night, so my fabulous mother-in-law (Wiggie) can get rest. He is a man of true integrity, and he is loved by so many. He is in so much pain now, and we all just want that pain to end. I love you, Roy Owings. You have meant so much to me in the years you've been a dad to me. Thank you for being you, and I know our lives will all have huge holes in them after you pass.

Chapter One

Wednesday, August 18th, 1852

I've lost all hope. My father died this morning, and I'm left with my three younger siblings to raise. After Mother died, Father had me start taking on all her normal tasks. I've been cooking, cleaning, and dealing with the children ever since. I'm only eighteen years old, and I now have three children to feed and no husband. What am I supposed to do?

For a moment—but only a moment—I thought of throwing myself onto the grave they'd dug for my father, right in the middle of the trail. At least Mother and Father will be reunited in death, as they are both buried along the same trail.

Now I must drive every day, mind the children, cook, and clean for them, and generally turn myself into both parents. I'm not sure how I can possibly meet all those demands, but I will if I must. I will just pray to my Maker, hoping he has not forsaken me. How can I trust a God who has put me into this terrible situation?

Sarah knelt on the trail beside her father's grave, which had no marker. They'd buried Father along the trail so the wagons would then run over it and no wild animals would dig it up, and Indians wouldn't find the grave to rob it. Not that there was anything to rob. They'd sold everything they owned to buy the oxen and the wagon for the oxen to pull.

Sarah sat in a small circle with Jack, Charles, and little Poppy. For many years after Sarah's birth, her mother had thought she'd become barren. And after ten years, she'd had three children in three years, and never had a child again.

Sarah felt the tears dripping down her face and saw them as they landed in the dirt of the trail. The dirt that would be her parents' permanent resting place.

Feeling a hand on her shoulder, Sarah wiped her tears from her face and looked behind her. "The captains have made the decision to stop for the day, and we'll resume tomorrow," Hannah, the preacher's wife, told her.

No one knew what had happened. Her father had been fine at breakfast, and by lunchtime he'd felt a little sickly. An hour before they usually stopped for the day, he'd fallen sideways out of the wagon, dead before he hit the ground.

Dr. Bentley said that was what cholera mostly did. It took a person from healthy to dead in a matter of hours at times. Father had refused to drink coffee all day long, preferring to have it only in the mornings. He'd taken to drinking water instead, and the water...well, it wasn't fit to drink, which they all knew, but Father...he'd assumed he was fine. He couldn't leave his four children alone, after all.

Sarah looked back at Hannah, who had become a close acquaintance along the walk. All the women had worked together to do so many things, and now...now Sarah was alone, but she was thankful for the friends she'd made along the way. "Thank you for letting me know."

Hannah squatted beside her, her belly sticking out for what seemed like four feet in front of her. "Would you like me to ask around for a young man to drive your wagon?"

Sarah nodded, looking at her siblings. "I don't know how I can drive, cook, clean, and care for them properly." Her only duties when they'd left Independence had been to help her mother with the meals and keep an eye out for the children.

"If you have to drive, the other women will make sure they don't get into trouble," Hannah said. "I'm hoping I can find someone. Mr. King's son is more than old enough to drive. I've seen him help some of the others out as people got sick along the way. I'll ask him if he can find it in his heart to help you out."

"Thank you, Hannah." It was the first time Sarah had used Hannah's given name, but before that moment, she'd felt as if she was a child, going along on her parents' journey west. Suddenly she felt as if she had the weight of the world on her shoulders, and she would be expected to do so much more than she had in her to do.

"You'll eat with my husband and I this evening," Hannah said. "We have some meat from the bear that was shot last night. I'll happily share with you."

"How long before we reach Oregon City?" Sarah asked. "I'm just ready for this journey to be over."

"Are you planning to settle near Oregon City?" Hannah asked.

Sarah knew most of the women in camp had all planned to live near Clover Creek, a section of the trail where they'd camped more than a month before. "I don't know what to do. I now must figure it all out on my own."

"You are among friends. We'll do all we can to help you, and I truly hope you'll settle with the rest of us. Then we'd know how best to help your family."

Sarah nodded. "I'll think on it." Though she had no idea what else she would do. Taking care of her family had to be her highest priority, but a little voice in her head asked, "What about your life? A husband? Children of your own." She ignored the voice. There was no choice. Her siblings wouldn't go to an orphanage when she was perfectly capable of caring for them. At least she hoped she was capable.

"I hope you really will. We're building a community here on the trail, and most of that community will be settling together. There's no reason for you not to accept the help that will be given."

Sarah sighed. "I thought about taking the children home to my grandmother, but there's no way we can handle another trip like this. Maybe I'll meet a wonderful man in Oregon City who won't mind taking on three children." She knew better, but positivity had always been a trait she'd admired.

Hannah smiled. "There are wonderful men out there. Just look at my Jed!"

Sarah tried to smile, but she simply couldn't make her face move that way. Losing two parents in a matter of months was too much for anyone.

Hannah returned to a standing position, and she held down a hand for Sarah. "Come with me. I'll fix some of that wonderful bear meat, and we'll have a small feast."

Sarah took the proffered hand and stood up, helping her brothers up as well. When Poppy threw her arms around Sarah, she lifted the little girl. "It's all going to be all right," she said, fully aware that she was lying. But she couldn't let her sister feel as terrible as she did.

As the four of them walked over to the Scotts' wagon, Elmer King walked toward them. He had a kind look on his face. "I'm so sorry for your loss. Would you like me to drive for you?"

Sarah blinked a couple of times before nodding. "Thank you, Mr. King."

"Mr. King is my father. Please, call me Elmer." He frowned for a moment. "Is there anything else I can do to help you out?" He looked at the two boys, walking along beside her, and the little girl in her arms. They all looked as if they'd spent the entire afternoon crying their hearts out. "Let me carry the little girl for you."

"I appreciate the thought, but Poppy is very much a shy child. She doesn't interact with people until she's been around them for a while."

"I see." Elmer walked along with her toward the Scotts' wagon. "Could we maybe walk after supper? I've been wanting to talk to you, but it never felt like the right time. Perhaps tonight?"

Sarah nodded, wiping her face with the back of her arm. "I suppose I can ask someone to mind the children for a little while, though I don't think I should be away from them for long. We just became orphans today, and it takes a bit out of you to realize you're suddenly on your own."

"I understand. Well, no I don't. Both of my parents are still alive, but my pa has made it clear that once we get to Oregon City, I'm on my own."

"But...You don't even have your own wagon? How could you possibly be on your own from there?"

He shrugged. "I have a little money saved, but not much. We'll talk."

Sarah nodded. "All right. After supper." She looked at Hannah who nodded.

"I'll mind the children. We'll play a game or something."

Jack pulled at Sarah's skirt. "Could we talk to the preacher about what happened instead?"

Hannah nodded emphatically. "If you want to talk, we'll talk. It's up to you!"

At Hannah's wagon, Sarah put Poppy down and looked at Hannah. "How can I help with supper?"

Hannah shook her head. "You buried your father today. Let me take care of supper."

While Hannah worked, Sarah sat with her siblings. "You know I'm going to take care of you all, right?"

Jack nodded. "You always do."

Poppy put her head in Sarah's lap. "Are you going to be my mama now?"

"I'll always be your sister, but now I'll be your sister who will take care of you all the time."

Poppy seemed confused still, but she nodded and closed her eyes, while Sarah ran her fingers through the little girl's hair. She knew it was something that calmed little Poppy, and she desperately wanted to help her any way she knew how. She had been pleased when Jack asked to speak with Pastor Scott. She wasn't sure if she could force out the words, "God will provide" even one more time. That's what her mother had said back in Independence. And after her mother passed, it was what her father said to her. She wasn't going to repeat the lie to her younger siblings. God obviously wasn't going to provide, so Sarah would have to rise to the occasion and provide for them and herself.

The four of them sat in a little circle, not speaking, but comforting each other without words. Sarah had been convinced her pain couldn't be any greater when her mother had died, and here she was, feeling double the pain she'd felt then.

When the meal was ready, Hannah gave them each a bowl. "It's just a bear stew, but I think it's pretty tasty."

Sarah smiled. "Thank you for feeding us. I'm sure it's wonderful."

As soon as they were finished eating, Sarah got to her feet. "I'll clean up," she said. If her hands were busy, perhaps her mind wouldn't do so much fretting over the future.

Hannah studied Sarah's face for a moment before nodding. "All right. I remember I was the same when my own father died. I wanted nothing more than to keep busy so I wouldn't have to think about anything."

Sarah tried again to smile, but she just couldn't do it. How could she smile just hours after her father had been buried?

Once the dishes were finished, Sarah spotted Elmer King walking her way. He walked straight to her. "Are you ready for that walk we talked about?"

"As ready as I'm going to be with the day we've had."

Elmer turned away from the circle of wagons, and led her out onto the trail, backtracking over the trail they'd already gone down. He waited until they were clear of the camp and past the camp guards before speaking. "I know what a terrible situation it must feel like you're in."

"I *am* in a terrible situation."

"I can't argue with that, but what if I present an alternative?" he asked softly.

She frowned at him. "What kind of alternative?"

"You're on your own with three mouths to feed. I'm about to be alone when we reach Oregon City in a couple of days. Why don't we marry? Then I won't have to spend all my money on a wagon and oxen. You'd have someone to not only drive your wagon but to help you raise your siblings."

"Are you serious?" she asked.

He nodded. "I know it's sudden, but I'm twenty-one. I know you're around the same age. It's natural for us both to be looking toward marriage. At least I think it is. I'm sure you think no one will marry you with an extra three mouths to feed, but I will. I've always wanted a large family, and you come with three ready-made children."

Her lips twitched at that. "Ready-made children?"

He shrugged. "I don't know how else to put it."

She pursed her lips, thinking about his offer. "I'm eighteen, just so you know. I...I don't even know what to say. You're right, I was thinking about never marrying because of my siblings. I do want to marry and have a family of my own, though I love my brothers and sister." She took a deep breath. "How about giving me a few days to think about it?"

"Sure. And I'll drive for you in the meantime. I'd like to know by Oregon City. If the answer is no, I'm going to have to buy supplies for myself and I won't be able to drive your wagon any longer. I guess if the answer is yes, I'll still need to get supplies."

"Could I tell you tomorrow evening? It would be good to think about it for at least twenty-four hours since there are five people involved and not just the two of us." Though how Sarah would be able to make such a monumental decision in such a short time, she didn't know.

He nodded. "I agree. Thinking about it is a good idea."

"What are you planning to do once we settle?" she asked. They had seen one another often, but she'd never spoken to him. He didn't seem to go to all the dances they had on Saturday nights. He was always at church though.

He sighed. "My father wants me to help him farmstead. We could have three times as much land if he, Mother, and I all choose adjoining plots of land for our homesteads. But I want to make furniture. I'm a craftsman, and I just finished an apprenticeship back in Pennsylvania. Now I want to be able to use all my training, but my father says I'm being disloyal."

Sarah nodded. "I understand both sides. My parents need me to take care of my siblings now, of course, but I want to have a life of my own. Every young girl dreams about getting married and having a home and family to take care of. Now I can't have that dream any longer. Instead, my entire station in life has completely changed."

Elmer held out his hand for Sarah. "I would be that husband. I'm a good man. I don't drink, and I don't smoke. I don't gamble. I don't even cuss. I'm a good Christian man who would stay by your side for the rest of my days."

Sarah took a deep breath. "We'll talk more tomorrow then." And she would make it her mission to talk to everyone in the entire company about him the next day. She wasn't going to drag her siblings into a horrible marriage.

Chapter Two

Thursday August 19th, 1852

I asked a young girl in my company, Sarah Wendt, to marry me after supper. No, I haven't been courting her, so it probably seems like a crazy thing to do. Part of the reason is my father's demand that I find my own way starting in Oregon City. The other part is Sarah's situation. Her mother died shortly after leaving Independence, and her father died yesterday. She has three younger siblings who must be cared for, and there is no one else to do it.

I've always liked the idea of a large family, and this will give us a head start with having children. She told me she will give me an answer tomorrow evening. She will probably ask others in camp about me, and I hope she does. She needs to know I am who I say I am.

Elmer stayed up much later than usual just watching the campfire burn. It was getting cold at night, and he chose to sleep under the stars right beside the fire. It kept him warm, and he felt safe by the fire. It gave him time to think about what he would need to buy for his woodworking shop. He'd get the full amount of land, and he would prove it up as required by law, but he wouldn't try to build a huge farming operation or a ranch. He would be too busy making his furniture.

He'd noticed that very close to Clover Creek there were trees. So many trees he could make into furniture. Much of it was pine, but there were other types as well. He couldn't wait to get his hands on some of that wood. Hopefully a lumber mill would be built in the area soon, but if not, he would cut the logs into boards himself. He had the skills. Now he just needed the tools.

If Sarah said yes, he could afford the tools. If she said no, he would need to purchase oxen, a wagon, and food for himself. He prayed she'd say yes. It would get them both out of a bind, but more than that, he would have a beautiful wife. He'd been admiring Sarah since they'd been camped in Independence, waiting to leave. He'd hoped to approach her soon, but her father dying had spurred him on.

He knew there were several widowers in the group, and if he didn't ask her to marry him, someone else would first. He couldn't let that happen.

He hugged his knees to his chest, just watching the fire. But why did all the flames take the shape of Sarah?

SARAH WOKE EARLY THE following morning, her mind in a mess. She'd just lost her father, but now she had an opportunity to be a wife. Elmer wouldn't have asked if it wasn't for her three siblings, but he was willing to accept them as his own. What did that say about him? More importantly, what did that say about *her*?

She made johnny cakes and bacon for breakfast. Her father had stashed money in the back of the wagon, so she could easily replenish supplies while they were in Oregon City. But should she buy supplies for four? Or for five?

She woke her siblings, putting her hand on them. "Time to wake up."

Charles woke up first. He looked so forlorn she wanted to cry for him, but she was relatively certain she was all cried out. Now she must survive. "Are you ready for another day? The captains said we should reach Oregon City tomorrow."

Charles shrugged. "I miss Father."

Sarah sighed. "I know you do. I do too." For a moment she thought about mentioning her marriage proposal to him, but he was much too young to help her decide. No, she'd work on that throughout the day, talking to all the women she knew. Maybe she'd even talk with Mrs. King, though in her mind, Elmer's parents were odious.

As her other siblings ate their breakfast, Charles kept playing with his. "What can I do to make you smile, Charles?" Sarah asked.

"I don't think there's anything anyone can do to make me smile. It's going to be a sad day. Do we have to walk far again?"

Sarah nodded. "We're not taking any more days off until we get back to Clover Creek. Tomorrow we'll all sign the papers for our land, but then we start walking again." And it occurred to her then she couldn't claim any land. She was under twenty-one. If she was married, she would count as old enough to get the land, but if not, they would soon have no land after walking so far.

"Can't we have a day off because our father died?" Jack asked, looking annoyed at the prospect of walking so far again.

Sarah shook her head. "That's just not possible."

Jack pouted, but he didn't ask again.

As soon as the breakfast dishes were done, Sarah packed up the back of the wagon, with some help from Jack. As the oldest of the three younger children, he tried hard to do his share.

About thirty minutes before it was time to head out, Elmer walked to their wagon. "Who wants to show me which oxen I should hitch up today?"

Jack shrugged. "I guess I can. I don't think it matters though because Father is dead, and we can't make it without him."

Sarah heard the words and decided then and there, if no one had something terrible to say about Elmer, she would marry him. She needed stability for the children, and if being married gave them that stability, then she would marry, and she would do it quickly.

She finished loading the wagon and took a last sip of her cold coffee. She'd never liked coffee, but since it was the difference between living and dying, she would drink it all day long. She only wished her father had been able to do the same.

When it was time to walk that day, Sarah found Hannah and told her what had transpired the previous evening. "I'm going to walk around and ask everyone who will talk to me what they know about Elmer King. I need to be sure he isn't the kind of man who will hurt the children."

Hannah frowned at the very idea. "I haven't heard anything negative, but when we stop for our noon break, I will ask Jed if he has. People would go to him before anyone else anyway."

"Will he answer that honestly?" Sarah asked.

"It depends on how I word it. If I ask him point blank if he's heard anything, he won't answer. But if I ask if there is any reason, he didn't think Elmer should marry someone with children, he will. Does that make sense?"

Sarah nodded. "Yes, please ask him. I'm ready to marry him tonight if no one says anything that frightens me."

Hannah went forward in the line, asking women what they knew about Elmer, while Sarah went backward, asking the same questions.

Sarah had talked to five women with no adverse comments when she reached Mrs. King. She was unsure if she should ask, but she knew it was important to her children, so she fought through the discomfort and asked.

"Mrs. King, is there any reason Elmer wouldn't be a good husband?"

Mrs. King shook her head. "Oh, my Isaiah is furious with him for not giving up on his idea of making furniture. For some reason that hard-headed husband of mine was convinced that if we all came west together, Elmer would decide to be a farmer like his father. It hasn't happened, so Isaiah is angry, and Elmer is sad. But that's between them. If I was you, I'd marry him right away."

Sarah nodded. "He doesn't have any bad habits or anything?"

"Well, now, you didn't ask me that. He forgets to wipe his feet and trudges dirt and snow on my clean floors. He doesn't put his dirty clothes in the laundry, instead they go on the floor of his bedroom. He argues with his pa because they're both too hardheaded for their own good." Mrs. King smiled. "You find a man who doesn't have bad habits, and I'll show you Jesus."

Sarah felt better and was very happy she'd spoken with his mother. Any mother who would admit to her son's bad habits would say if there was something that should keep him from marrying. She was sure of it.

By the noon meal, she was convinced. Unless Jed said something negative, then she'd marry Elmer. It would take a huge weight off her shoulders, and she would feel safe regarding the future. As safe as one could feel marrying a total stranger that is.

Mary caught up with her. "I'm so sorry about your father!"

Sarah nodded. "Thank you." She had no idea how to respond to that, but she'd heard it so much since they'd begun the trail west.

"I hear you're thinking about marrying Elmer. He and my Bob have become good friends."

"Oh? Do you have anything negative to tell me about Elmer?"

"I don't think there is anything negative *to* tell you. He's a nice man. I've talked to him a few times, and I can't say anything bad. Neither could Bob. I asked him."

"How did you ask while he's driving?" Sarah asked.

Mary grinned. "I walked up beside the wagon and climbed in. No big deal."

Sarah couldn't help but smile. Mary didn't think anything was hard as far as Sarah could see. The other girl had proven to be an absolute marvel. It was she who had brought down the bear just two days before. It had fed the entire camp twice over.

"Easy for you."

"Yes!" Mary kicked a rock out of their path. "Anyway, I think he'd make a good husband and a good father to your brothers and sister. And I would tell you if I didn't think it was a good idea."

"That much I know about you. You are not afraid to speak your mind."

"That's a good trait, right?"

Sarah just smiled, thinking Mary could make of that whatever she liked.

Shortly after their noon break was over, Hannah rushed over to Sarah. "Jed said he's heard nothing but positive things about Elmer. You should marry him."

"That's all I've heard from anyone. Even his mother told me that he's a wonderful man. She told me all of his bad habits, too."

Hannah laughed. "You know she told you the truth then."

"I'm sure she did. I guess I'm getting married this evening. I'd like to have it out of the way before we reach Oregon City."

"Jed will happily do that for you. And tomorrow, we finally get to see the elephant!"

Sarah nodded. "I didn't think it would ever happen. Losing both of my parents along the way wasn't something I was expecting."

"I know. But it'll all work out in the end."

"I just have to have faith, right?" Sarah tried to keep the sarcasm from her voice, but it was difficult. How could she trust God when he'd allowed her parents to die, and put so much more on her than she could handle?

Hannah frowned. "Do you need to talk to Jed? Are you angry with God?"

Sarah nodded.

"I was when my father died, and even madder at him when my mother married my stepfather. Now, though, I realize that if all of that hadn't happened, I never would have married my Jed, and I believe with everything inside me that I was meant to marry him. And have a child. I just wish I knew if it would be a boy or a girl."

"I can say a definite yes to that!"

Hannah looked confused for a moment, but then she grinned at Sarah. "I forget about your sense of humor sometimes, but I'm happy to see it's still there. Even after tragedy."

Sarah looked around. "I need to go find my siblings and let them know I'm marrying."

"I saw Charles and Jack a ways back talking to some of the Mitchell kids."

"And I'm going to guess that Poppy is with the little girls who always walk together." Sarah realized that for the first time that day, she hadn't kept an eye on her siblings. She'd been too worried about getting information about Elmer.

Hannah nodded. "Go talk to them."

Sarah hurried and found Jack and Charles, and then Jack ran for Poppy. The four siblings walked together, and Sarah told them her plan. "You all know Mr. King, right? The one who's driving our wagon?"

Jack nodded. "I helped him find the oxen this morning."

"Thank you for that. I want to let you all know that Mr. King has asked me to marry him, and I'm going to say yes."

"Does that mean I won't have to be the man of the family anymore?" Jack asked.

Sarah nodded. "He wouldn't be your new father. Instead, he'd be your brother-in-law, but he would help me raise you and put food on the table."

Jack smiled. "I'm so relieved! I was going to have to quit school and do all the planting and milking by myself."

"No, you were not. But I'm glad you're pleased I'm marrying Elmer."

Poppy wrinkled her nose. "Elmer is a funny name."

"Well, don't tell him that!" Sarah said. "We're going to get married by the pastor tonight, and tomorrow we finally reach Oregon City, where we can stake our claims."

"Father wanted to get to Oregon City really bad," Charles said.

"He did. But now we'll go, and he'll look down on us from heaven and be happy we did what he couldn't do." Sarah hated bringing heaven into the discussion with the way she was feeling about God, but she knew it would comfort her siblings. "Before supper, we'll go and ask Pastor Scott to marry us. Does that sound like a good plan to you?"

Poppy jumped up and down, clapping her hands. "Can I be the flower girl."

Sarah frowned. "I don't think the wedding will be formal, but sure. You can hold flowers."

"Do you think we can find some poppies?"

"I don't think so. We'll just find some pretty wildflowers for you to carry."

Poppy sighed. "Mother should have named me Daisy. I see daisies all the time!" With that, the little girl ran back to her friends.

"All right. You two go and do whatever you're going to do."

Jack smiled. "The Cauldron boys are going to teach us something this afternoon."

Sarah closed her eyes for a moment. "I'm not sure that's such a great idea." The Cauldron boys were known to be the worst behaved children in the company.

Charles laughed. "They're our friends!" And the boys were gone.

Sarah took a deep breath and walked quickly to catch up with her wagon. She needed to tell Elmer what they'd decided.

Chapter Three

Thursday, August 19th, 1852

Yesterday my father died, and last night, an entire new world opened up to me. One of the young men who had come along with his parents asked me to be his bride. The reasons are more practical than anything else, but he has agreed to help me raise my siblings, and I have agreed to cook his meals for him.

I barely know the young man, but I have asked all around the company about him, and everyone has expressed that he is a wonderful person and will be a good father-figure to my siblings. They are the most important thing right now. Not my feelings or lack thereof.

We will be married by Pastor Scott this evening, and Poppy has requested that she may be the flower girl. From what people are saying, we will reach Oregon City before noon tomorrow, all will stake claims and restock their wagons. Then we will start heading home to Clover Creek.

Just yesterday I was fretting about how I was going to make it with no one to help with my siblings, and today, I feel like I have a right to celebrate a bit. Maybe I'm not in love with Elmer, but I can still choose to love him every day, and that's what I shall do.

Sarah hurried up beside the wagon and climbed up while it was still moving. It was much easier than she'd thought it would be, and she wondered why more women didn't do it.

Elmer was startled to see her appear in the seat next to him, but he couldn't help but grin. "Did Bob's wife teach you to do that?"

Sarah laughed. "As a matter of fact, she did!"

He chuckled. "I know I've seen other women do the same thing, but I have no doubt Mary is the first of the women to do it, and she must have taught all the others."

"I do believe you're right about that." Sarah thought for a moment to come up with the right words. "I've been asking about you all over camp today, and I've concluded that you are exactly what you seem to be. A kind man who wants to marry me and help with my siblings."

"This is true."

"So, I'm going to marry you this evening. Poppy has decided to be my flower girl. She didn't understand that I won't really need one, but that's all right by me. She's a good girl." Sarah realized she was jabbering, and she knew it was because she was nervous. "I guess you don't need to buy a wagon after all."

His grin completely transformed his face from average to handsome. "No, I guess I won't. I will be buying some tools then. I couldn't bring many with me."

"That's all right. We'll find a place for them in the wagon. We'll want to move all your belongings into our wagon tonight after the wedding. Pastor Scott has said he'll marry us before supper."

"Good work getting things set up. Have you told the children yet?"

"Yes, that's why Poppy wants to be my flower girl."

He laughed softly. "I was so excited that you agreed to marry me, I suppose I wasn't paying attention to all the details."

She smiled. "I'll start a stew as soon as we get to camp tonight, and then after the wedding, it should be ready to eat."

"How much food do you need tomorrow?" he asked

"Well, since Father died, I'll have his portion. We've had more than most already since Mother died so early in the journey. I'll want fresh flour and fresh cornmeal. Fresh bacon. Any jerky we can find. I'm not only thinking about what we'll need on the way back to Clover Creek but also what we'll need for the winter."

"I hadn't thought about the winter," Elmer said, shaking his head. "Do you have money to buy the food we'll need?"

"Yes, I do. Father showed me where he kept the money hidden, and I have plenty for us to have food. Do you have what you need?"

"Yes, I just need to buy a few tools. I can't buy a lot because they won't fit in the wagon."

She frowned at that. "Will you be able to make your own?"

"That's my plan," he said smiling at her. "I will buy just enough tools to be able to make my own. I won't be able to start doing much carpentry until the house is built anyway. Maybe I'll cut down a few of the mountain mahogany trees and play with those during the winter. I think I'll have to spend most of my time finishing the house though. Then in the spring, we'll plant enough crops to satisfy the government."

"Sounds good to me." She liked that he had plans she was now a part of. "We're going to need a decent sized house since we're starting our marriage with five people."

"I can handle that. I'm very good with wood."

"It sounds like you really know what you're doing." Sarah looked straight ahead, and she realized that far in the distance, there were more houses along the way. They were close to Oregon City, and the goal they'd been marching toward since spring. Soon they would have their claims. It hadn't really felt real to Sarah until that moment. "Are we going to get a double portion of land since we'll be married when we arrive there?"

"I was hoping so. Then we can chop trees on our property. I'm hoping to be outside of Clover Creek a little where I'll have more access to trees. There's a huge forest close to there, but not as close as I think most will want to settle."

"Will I be able to see my friends with an hour or two of driving?"

"Oh, most definitely," he told her. "I don't plan to be far from the settlement."

"I wonder if you could start a business cutting down trees for farmers. Then you could use the wood for your own purposes." Sarah was always looking for ways to make some extra money.

"I don't think I'll need to, but I could."

"All right. Then we'll see how things go." She looked at the ground. "I don't know how you ride in this wagon. It feels like I'm being thrown every which way." As soon as the words were out of her mouth, an uneven bit of land had her thrown against Elmer. "I'm sorry!"

He put an arm around her. "I'm not. You're going to be my wife tonight. Why wouldn't I want you to touch me?"

Sarah blushed and looked down. "I think I'll go see how the women are doing."

He chuckled. "You don't have to be shy around me."

"I don't know how not to be." With those words, she jumped off the slow-moving wagon and walked back to where the other women were walking.

Trudie waved to her. "How are you doing today?"

Sarah smiled slightly. "I'm all right. I'm getting married tonight."

"Married?" Trudie asked. "Then I am making your wedding supper. Everyone helped me so much when I was first married, that I want to help others. I don't know what it will be yet, but I'll tell Mary I need something special."

"To Mary, squirrels are something special. I have no desire to eat squirrel stew."

Trudie laughed. "No squirrel stew. How about baked potatoes with butter?"

Sarah smiled. "That sounds delicious."

"I'll try to get some good meat to go with it, but if I don't, baked potatoes are filling." Trudie hurried off to talk to Mary, and Sarah found herself walking alone for a bit.

When they made camp that evening, Sarah immediately changed into a dress she'd worn to parties back east. Two women held up blankets on either side of her so she wouldn't be seen. Sarah would never get used to the lack of privacy on the trail. The first time all the other women had surrounded her, holding their skirts out so she could urinate right there beside the trail, it had struck her as odd. Now she just expected it to happen.

When she was dressed, Sarah looked at Hannah, who had been holding out a blanket to cover her. "What do you think?"

Hannah smiled. "I think you should wear that dress more often. It's very fetching. That blue brings out the color of your eyes. I never noticed they were blue until you put that on."

"Thank you." Sarah hadn't felt the need to dress up while on the trail. What was the point? She was just going to get dirty anyway.

Elmer joined her as soon as he'd finished taking care of the oxen. "Are we ready?" he asked.

Sarah looked around for her siblings. Poppy came running toward her with a fistful of flowers she'd found. Jack and Charles joined them, and Jack made a show of sizing up Elmer. "Are you going to be good to my sister and always treat her well?"

Elmer bit back a smile. "I will always be good to her."

"Then I give you permission to marry her and give up the duty of being the man of the family." Jack looked so earnest that Sarah did her best not to smile.

"Thank you for being man of the family for us," she said, hugging her younger brother. "Now, let's go get married!"

Sarah was surprised to see his parents join them at Hannah and Jed's wagon, but she smiled at Mrs. King. "Thank you for coming."

"I'm going to watch my only child get married. I told Mr. King he could come with me or get his own supper tonight."

Sarah bit back a laugh. Mrs. King was someone special, and she would be proud to call her family.

The wedding was quick, and when Jed told Elmer he may kiss the bride, Sarah was surprised when he did it. She'd expected a kiss on the cheek, but instead, he kissed her lips, and held her close for just a moment longer than was proper.

People all around them congratulated them. Sarah was surprised at the sheer amount of people who had come to their little last-minute wedding ceremony.

Trudie waved them over. "Mary didn't get anything, but Joseph got a deer yesterday, so I'll just use that meat. We shared with a few, but it wasn't a buck, so we didn't pass food to everyone."

Sarah nodded. "I understand."

"So, we're having a venison roast and baked potatoes for supper."

"That sounds wonderful. Thank you."

Elmer looked at Sarah in surprise. "I thought you were going to make stew."

"Trudie offered to cook our supper as a wedding present."

"Thank you." Elmer was thrilled people were gathering to help Sarah. With everything she'd been through on the journey, he felt like she should have received a great deal of help, but his mother had explained that they all needed help.

Trudie smiled. "You're very welcome. I made a little gravy out of the drippings, and I thought it might be nice on the baked potatoes."

"That sounds wonderful," Sarah said. "I'm sure the children will love it. Thank you for taking the time to cook for us when you didn't have to. It is much appreciated."

Trudie delivered the food to Sarah's wagon, and the five of them sat to eat together for the first time as a family.

"We all need to thank Mrs. Simmons for cooking for us tonight," Sarah told the children.

"I'll say the prayer," Elmer offered.

They ate the meal happily. Sarah realized with her first bite that Trudie was a much better cook than she was, and she prided herself on her cooking.

As soon as the meal was over, Elmer went to his parents' wagon and brought his own things to add to her wagon. "We will probably have to make sure that all rotten food gets thrown away tomorrow," he said, looking at the space available. "Perhaps we can go through everything and get rid of some things that we won't need."

She nodded. "I haven't disposed of even my mother's things yet, though Father told me to. I suppose we can go through and get rid of his things as well as her things. It will free up space."

"Maybe while we're in the city tomorrow," he suggested. "I can't believe how excited I am to see a town. It's been far too long."

"Did you live in a town in Pennsylvania?" she asked, and he shook his head.

"No, we were in the country there, but we didn't have enough land for a decent farm. That's why we're taking advantage of the government land."

She nodded. "That makes sense."

"What about your parents? What were their dreams of living out west?"

Sarah thought about it for a moment. "Pa wanted to have a ranch. Fourteen of the oxen are ours. We can breed them or use them for meat and milk. I'm not fussy about them."

"I can use them to help me drag logs back to our homestead." Elmer was surprised at how excited he was to have several oxen to choose from.

"Oh good. I don't want them killed right away for meat, though I know we'll need to use some of them for food for the winter."

"We'll see how that goes," he said. "I may be able to bring in enough game that we'll be fine. I'm a good shot. Maybe not as good as Bob's wife, but good."

Sarah laughed. "No one needs to be as good as Mary."

Together they loaded the wagon with Elmer's things, finding space easily since they were down on provisions. They'd only bought enough to get them to Oregon City, and they knew they'd buy more once they arrived.

When that task was finished, he smiled at her. "Who can watch the children while we go for a nice long walk?"

Sarah was surprised he wanted to walk. "I already walked twenty-five miles today. Why are we going for a long walk?" It made no sense to her at all.

"I thought we'd take a blanket, and we can have our wedding night."

Sarah's eyes widened. "But we don't have that kind of marriage. We married for the children."

Elmer frowned. "You married for the children. I married for many reasons, one of them was being able to touch you the way I've wanted to touch you."

Sarah felt panicked at the suggestion. "I...I don't think I am ready for that. Her mother had talked to her about her wedding night, but she hadn't realized Elmer expected one.

"You didn't expect a wedding night?"

"No, I really didn't. Can we get to know each other for a week or two before a wedding night?"

"One week. I don't like it, but I can wait a week."

Sarah breathed a sigh of relief, walking to Elmer and wrapping her arms around him. "Thank you."

He was obviously disappointed, and she felt badly for making him feel that way, but she just wasn't ready. A week should be enough time.

Chapter Four

Friday, August 20th, 1852

I married Sarah Wendt last night, and I was so looking forward to a wedding night with her. I've had feelings for her since I saw her across the campground in Independence, helping her mother with their family's supper. I couldn't get up the courage to ask her to dance with me, so I didn't go to the dances held every Saturday night.

She only married me so she would have someone to help her raise her young siblings after the death of both parents on the trail. I married her because I wanted to help, but more than anything, I married her because I've had feelings for her for a very long time.

She didn't expect a wedding night to occur, and I don't know why she didn't because we talked of having more children. Where did she think they'd come from? I must now wait a week for her to be ready for a wedding night. I think I can last that long, but only if I don't sleep beside her. Sarah is everything to me and having her as my wife is a dream come true. Now I just need to convince her to love me, and all will be good. At least I hope it will.

We are camped on the bank of the Willamette River, a half day's walk from Oregon City, where we will all stake our claims. I cannot believe we are this close to Trail's End. Of *course, we must walk another month yet as we find the exact spot we want to settle, which is a spot where we camped for two nights, back near Clover Creek.*

I'm filled with a strange mixture of disappointment as well as excitement. Our new lives will start when we reach the claims we will file for tomorrow. The disappointment is only due to the lack of a wedding night, but I'm certain any red-blooded man would feel the same about that.

I cannot wait to settle down with my family and do what I've trained to do for the past few years. I will make furniture.

Elmer spotted Sarah mixing something up for breakfast. It was strange to think he would eat her cooking for the first time. He was certain she was a good cook because she'd made meals for her family before her mother passed.

He closed his journal and walked to sit beside her. "What are you making?"

She jumped. "Oh, you frightened me. The children never wake on their own, so I never speak to anyone until I wake them."

He smiled. "I'm sorry to give you a fright. I was just writing in my journal, and I saw you fixing breakfast, so I thought I'd come over here and wish you good morning."

Sarah smiled at him. "Thank you. I will remember that you're an early riser as well and not get frightened again. How was it sleeping with the boys last night?" She had asked him to sleep under the wagon with her brothers, while she continued to sleep with Poppy. She hadn't been ready to sleep beside him.

"It wasn't too bad. Charles woke me up making some sounds in the middle of the night, but Jack said that's just what he does."

Sarah nodded emphatically. "He has always done that. I remember one night before we left home, he let out a scream in the middle of the night. Mother and I were certain he'd broken a bone or something, but he was still sleeping. I still wonder what that scream had been about."

"Hopefully that won't happen with me there. I'm afraid I'd go for my pistol and not even stop to think about what was wrong." Elmer shook his head. "Are you looking forward to finally reaching Oregon City?"

"Some. I know a few families will part with us when we leave in the morning. The Cauldrons will go to a settlement northeast of us. The Blues will go north of here. I'm sure there are others I'm forgetting. Who will entertain us at the dances without Edna Blue?"

"Is Edna that young woman who walks around looking like she's in a cloud and has no idea what's happening around her?" Elmer asked.

"That would be her. I can say her dancing is unparalleled by anyone else in camp." Sarah couldn't help but smile as she thought of the girl.

"I wish I'd seen it!"

"You never went to the dances. Why not?"

Elmer shrugged. "I didn't think the only lady in camp I wanted to dance with was interested."

Sarah was surprised at his words. "Who did you want to dance with?" *And why did you marry me and not her?*

"It was you. I couldn't get up the nerve to ask you for a dance, or a walk, so I stayed away, praying no other man would ask you to dance."

She blinked a few times. "No one ever did." At the time, it had hurt her feelings that no one wanted to dance with her. *Why did God answer his prayers and not mine?*

Elmer kissed her cheek softly. "They're all blind fools."

"You really wanted to dance with me?"

"I did. I wish I'd asked."

"I would have said yes," Sarah said softly.

"Now I *really* wished I'd asked." He looked at the mixing bowl in her hands. "What are you making for breakfast?"

"Johnny cakes. My brothers and sister love them, so I try to make them every morning. If you want something else, just let me know, and I'll be sure to make it."

"Thank you," he said. "I'll try your johnny cakes."

"Your mother didn't make them?" she asked.

"My pa didn't think they were good enough to eat, so she's been making us eggs for breakfast. She brought along eight chickens, and that was enough eggs for all three of us to have every single morning."

"Your pa sounds like a difficult man to be around."

"Oh, trust me. He is. I'm sure you'll get to know him, as they plan on settling in Clover Creek with the rest of the company."

Sarah smiled. "Well, you let me know what you like for breakfast. I don't mind making one thing for the children, and something else for the two of us."

"My mother said the same thing, and then my pa yelled at me about how I'm making more work for her. I'm sure I'll be happy with johnny cakes."

"They're good if you serve them with butter and honey. I'll fix yours for you the first time, so you can see why we love them so much."

"All right! And then the next time I can put more butter or more honey on them based on my own tastes. Perfect." Elmer stretched. "I'm going to take a walk around the campground, and I'll be back in a few minutes. I'm ready to try something new."

"Sounds good!"

As he walked away, Sarah thought about what he'd said. He'd wanted to ask her to dance for that long? It seemed impossible.

She poured the first round of johnny cakes and called the children. When she called each of them by name, they tended to wake faster, so that's what she did. "Jack, Charles, Poppy! Breakfast!"

She flipped each of the small cakes.

As her siblings came out, they each took a plate and the butter she'd made, and they piled on the toppings they liked. While she cooked for her and Elmer, they ate their breakfast, talking nonstop about what it would be like to be in a city after so long.

"You three will need to go to the land office with us, so I can keep an eye on you. After, we'll go to the store and get some more food. I'm going to need to clean out the wagon today as well, so I'd like all three of you to help with that."

Poppy pouted. "You're making us work? Did you forget our father just died?"

"That's not going to work, Poppy. My father just died as well, and if I didn't work, you wouldn't eat."

Jack grinned at his younger sister. "Good try, though. I bet it would have worked on Mother."

"But not on me," Sarah said, flipping the last of the johnny cakes onto two plates, covering each with butter and honey.

Just as she'd finished, Elmer walked into camp. "Is one of those for me?" he asked.

"Absolutely. I like making pancakes a lot, but cornmeal lasts longer." Sarah felt bad that the first meal she made for her new husband was simple johnny cakes, but perhaps he'd be happy that he didn't have to eat with his father.

Elmer sat on the ground beside Sarah and took her hand as he prayed over the meal. Her siblings looked stunned for a moment before they lowered their heads.

After the prayer, Jack looked at Sarah in shock. "You forgot to have us pray!"

Sarah shrugged. "Perhaps I did." She hadn't forgotten though. She'd chosen not to. God had taken her parents from her, and she had no desire to praise him for anything or ask for anything. No, she was *angry* with God.

As soon as breakfast was over, Elmer looked over at Sarah. "Before I go to hitch up the wagon, I want to tell you that I think johnny cakes are my new favorite breakfast." He kissed her softly, tasting the honey on her lips. "Oregon City or bust!"

He stood up and Jack walked with him to help him choose the oxen. He was getting used to helping Elmer the way he had their father, and Sarah was proud of him. She was also just a little bit flustered by Elmer's kiss. Her parents had never kissed in full view of their children, but Elmer didn't seem to care who was around when he had a mind to kiss her. She wasn't sure if she should scold him or enjoy his kisses.

Poppy helped her with the breakfast dishes with no complaints while Charles reloaded everything into the wagon.

When Jack and Elmer came back to camp with the oxen, Sarah nodded her thanks. "It's going to be good to restock today. I'm excited about this trip!"

"I am too," Elmer said. "And I'm buying some tools."

"Is there any way I can help with that?" Sarah asked.

He shook his head. "No, but if you would take care of purchasing the food we need, that would help me a great deal."

"The children and I will need to throw some of the supplies away. We'll do that after I shop, and we'll make sure to leave you plenty of room for your tools." Along the journey they'd all seen many things they would have liked to take along the trail. There was no room, though, and that's why the other emigrants had thrown them out as well.

Elmer rubbed his hands together. "Do you have any idea how excited I am to be able to work doing what I want to do once we reach Clover Creek?"

She smiled and nodded. "I think I do. But shelter first!"

"I know. We will all need to have somewhere to sleep that's warm and dry before the snows." He put the iron skillet she'd used for breakfast into the back of the wagon. "You're welcome to come see me on the wagon seat whenever you need a quick break from walking."

"Thank you. I may take you up on that." Sarah was surprised when Elmer walked to her and kissed her. "You don't mind people can see us kissing?"

Elmer laughed. "I don't care at all if people see us. I just like kissing you, and I'm going to keep doing it."

"All right." She watched as he climbed into the wagon seat, and soon they were rolling away from camp.

She fell in with the other women and children. The excitement in the camp was almost palpable. Everyone was talking as if they hadn't seen one another for months, even though they'd been together every step along the way—and it had been a lot of steps. It was good to feel the happiness. They had almost made it to Oregon City, the destination they'd all dreamed about.

Sarah felt as if there would be streets paved of gold when they arrived. She'd heard many tales about how it would be in Oregon. There would be so many fish, they would jump out of the river, and put themselves in your skillet, already cleaned. She knew better of course, but it almost felt like the land should be magical.

For a moment as she walked, she allowed herself to daydream. What if the animals that they would need to hunt would be lining either side of the trail as they walked into Oregon City? Maybe there would be people in the streets singing to welcome them.

She chuckled out loud and was startled to realize someone was walking by her side. "You certainly look happy this morning," Hannah said.

Sarah grinned, explaining the daydream she'd just had. "So, while I know it's all silliness, I could picture it happening."

Hannah nodded. "That would be a sight for sure." She kept watching Sarah as they walked. "How's married life?" Hannah finally asked.

Sarah smiled. "It's good. He's a kind man." Sarah looked to see if anyone else was close enough to hear their conversation. "I thought he was just marrying me, so he'd have a wagon to get back to Clover Creek," she whispered. "But he expected to have a wedding night."

"Oh, dear. How did you settle it?"

"He's agreed to wait a week, and he's being very good-natured about it. He slept with my brothers last night and didn't even complain about the odd noises Charles makes in his sleep."

"He's a good man," Hannah said simply. "You're going to be very thankful for him by winter, I think."

"I'm already thankful for him. He's driving my wagon. He's good with my siblings, and he says he's been attracted to me since Independence." Sarah shook her head. "I don't see how that's possible. He's never asked me to walk with him. He's never asked me to dance. Why would he wait so long to try to court me?"

Hannah shrugged. "Perhaps he was shy."

"Perhaps. But why now then?" she asked.

"There are other men without wives in this group. He was probably afraid you'd marry someone else, simply to have help with your siblings. Your father dying made you much more eligible to the other men, because they would all know you needed help."

"I hadn't thought of it that way. Well, I'm still glad that I'm married to Elmer and not someone else."

Hannah nodded. "I am as well. I think the two of you are going to be very happy together."

Chapter Five

Friday, August 20th, 1852

We did it! We made it to Oregon City today, and while the streets are not made of gold and no one is singing in the streets welcoming us, I do believe I'm quite pleased with all we accomplished today, not the least of which was getting our land.

I have restocked supplies and cleaned out the wagon, passing Mother and Father's clothing to other families in the company. I kept little that belonged to them, but I did keep Mother's old Bible with the family tree in the back. Someday, I will be happy to have that information at my fingertips.

While Oregon City is by no means a place I would call civilized, I'm thankful it's where we went to get our land. There were stores, and I was able to buy some tea, so I wouldn't have to drink cold coffee for every single meal.

Elmer was pleased with the tools he purchased, and he believes he can make the rest of the things he wants, so that is a plus. Also there's a family in our company who is planning to open a general store once we reach our land. Just think! No more are we talking about making it to Oregon City. Now we want to reach our land. It will take us over a month, but that seems like such a short time, seeing as we left Independence back in March.

Soon, I'll have a home. No more cooking over a campfire. No more waking up on the ground. We'll have our very own home, and I will have Elmer at my side. I was unsure how I felt about him at first, but he is really starting to mean a great deal to me. I believe I'll keep him around.

It was shortly before eleven in the morning when they walked into Oregon City. It wasn't a bustling city by any means, but it had what they so desperately needed, and that's what mattered to all the emigrants.

Before they took time to eat their lunches, Elmer and Sarah, along with the children, stood in line at the land office. Sarah was shocked at how quickly the line went, and she stood silently while he found the plots they wanted and signed for them.

They left with the paperwork for the land, and it was all Sarah could do not to dance her way out onto the street. There was going to be a future for her and her family after all.

The afternoon was spent doing many things. Sarah fixed a quick lunch, and then she went through the wagon, making a pile of her mother's clothes as well as her father's Afterward, she went through the camp and asked people if they would use them. The Mitchell family ended up taking them, which was good, because they had more people than should ever be in just one family.

After the clothes were distributed, she went back to the wagon to look at her food stores. She'd had a vague idea she should probably throw some things out, but as she looked, she realized it was more than she'd thought.

They'd camped outside of town, so she and her brothers put all the food that was no longer viable onto the ground, and then she and all three siblings headed to the general store in town for more food.

She purchased a twenty-five-pound bag of rice, a fifty-pound-bag of beans, a large bag of potatoes, coffee, tea, sugar, flour, and cornmeal.

She even purchased a large jar of honey for their johnny cakes in the mornings. When the merchant offered to have everything delivered to the encampment after they closed at five, she wanted to kiss him in thanks. She had a feeling Elmer wouldn't be pleased, though, so she just thanked him profusely, paying for the items with some of the money her parents had received from selling all their belongings before they'd left for Independence.

Sarah hadn't realized how much money was left, but she was pleased to see she still had money after buying the food she thought they would need, both for the journey home, and for the winter ahead.

As they walked back to camp, her purse was lighter, but her smile was brighter. They were going to be able to make it now. She'd even purchased some bacon and salt pork, so they would have meat on those days when game was scarce. Finally, it felt as if her luck was changing, but she wished it had happened before she'd lost both parents.

Back at camp, Mary had spent the afternoon hunting, and gotten two deer. They shared with the camp, and Sarah immediately went to help dry the meat. There was enough for everyone to have a meal from the animals, and then there would be three more meals with the dried meat. Sarah felt blessed to receive some fresh meat to go with all the food she'd purchased.

Elmer came back to camp without anything in his hands, and she wondered if something had happened, but she decided he must have asked for everything to be delivered, just as she had.

Elmer looked in the back of the wagon, and his eyes widened. "There's not much left!"

"I got rid of all the food that needed to go. I gave away my parents' clothes and other belongings. I only kept my mother's Bible for the family tree she'd written into the back. And I kept her music box, because it was her favorite thing."

"Were you able to purchase food?" he asked, suddenly worried they wouldn't have enough food to make it home.

"Yes! It will be delivered after the store closes. What about you? Did you find the tools you need?"

He nodded. "All except for one thing, and I didn't quite have enough money for that."

"Do you need it?" she asked.

"Well, yes, but I suppose it will have to wait."

She led him back to her wagon and pulled out the remainder of the money her parents had. "If there's room in the wagon for the tool you're thinking about, here's a little more money."

She handed him several coins, and his eyes widened. "Are you sure?" he asked. He didn't feel right taking money from her family.

She stepped close to him, lowering her voice. "I know I disappointed you last night. Perhaps this will make up for it at least a little. Besides, we're married. Everything I own is technically yours."

He let out a loud whoop, and wrapped his arms around her, picking her right up off her feet and spinning her in a slow circle. "Thank you!" He kissed her quickly and then let her go abruptly, hurrying back toward town. He needed to get there before the store closed.

Sarah just laughed and started their campfire. It was still hotter than she would have liked, but she supposed it was better than being cold. She put on what little rice they had left and then she cooked the fresh meat Mary had given to her. She would cut it up, use the drippings to make gravy, and serve the gravy over the rice. Thankfully, there was more rice coming.

She hummed to herself as she cooked, feeling a little ashamed when she realized what she was doing. She'd only lost her father two days ago, and she was already acting as if nothing had happened.

The deliveries came just before supper. Sarah sent the children to pick up the order that said, "King," on it. It was so strange to use someone else's name. She wondered for a moment why women changed their last name when they married instead of men, but then brushed the thought aside.

Elmer came back into camp, carrying a large wood and metal thing. Sarah could only assume it was the tool he'd wanted to buy before they headed toward Clover Creek.

He dropped the tool beside her and ran back to the delivery wagon to help the children, without even saying a word.

Sarah sighed happily. Never in her wildest imagination would she have thought she would marry a man who would do household tasks without having to be asked six times. She really had made a good decision when she'd married Elmer.

She had food on five plates by the time Elmer and the children returned to the wagon with their purchases. "We have to go back for more," Elmer said as he set the things he carried on the ground. All three children followed suit and hurried back to the delivery wagon with Elmer.

While she waited for her family, Sarah began the task of putting the supplies in the back of the wagon. She'd kept her mother's set up for the wagon, but now as she reloaded it, she did things in a way that made sense to her.

Elmer and the children were able to bring all the supplies back in the next load, and Elmer and Jack went back for the remainder of his tools.

Sarah got Charles and Poppy situated with their suppers while the tools were brought back. Elmer took his plate and sat down, as Jack set the last tool up against a wagon wheel.

"Do you want to load the wagon with my help? Or do you want me to decide where everything goes?" Elmer asked after their prayer.

"I'd like to do that if it's all right. I've kept the wagon the way my mother set it up in Independence, even though her organization made no sense to me. I've thought all afternoon about how I want it differently this time, and I'd like to be the one doing the organizing." Sarah was unsure how Elmer would feel about her doing it. Her father had always had things he thought he should do and things he wouldn't do, and her mother would have to. Sometimes those things made sense to Sarah and sometimes they didn't.

After the dishes were done, Sarah climbed into the back of the wagon, where there was room now that she'd gotten rid of so many things. Elmer and Jack took turns handing things to her, and she would put them where she wanted them. They had packed lightly for their trip, and there was no furniture to get in the way. They had clothes for the five of them, food, and now Elmer's tools. The wagon wasn't nearly as full as she'd been afraid it would be. "Perhaps I should have bought another bag of rice," she said, pursing her lips.

Elmer laughed, putting his hands at her waist, and lifting her to the ground. "I'm certain we have enough rice."

The children asked to play with their friends that evening, and Sarah was happy to allow them to go. She was tired. They hadn't done nearly as much walking as usual that day, but she'd shopped and gone to the land office after her half-day walk.

Elmer sat with his back to a large rock, and pulled Sarah down to sit beside him, his arm going about her shoulders. "I think we accomplished a lot today," he said softly.

"We did. I'm very excited to get settled into our land now," she said. "I bought a big piece of fabric that I'll use for tablecloths and curtains. I've never had a home of my own, and I will for the first time."

"Won't that be fun?" he asked. "I want to build myself a large workshop where I can build the furniture I want to sell. Would you mind if I taught Jack to make furniture, so he'll have a trade when he's grown?"

Sarah smiled, snuggling closer to him. She was surprised at how much she enjoyed being close to Elmer. "I think that would be wonderful. But if he doesn't like it, he doesn't have to continue. Same thing with Charles, though he's only seven and Jack is eight."

"Your siblings are so much younger than you!"

"My mother thought she was barren after me. She had no children for ten years, and then she had three, three years in a row. And none since. And now she'll never have more."

"But we will. We'll raise our children and your parents'. I'm looking forward to the day that I can start the work I prefer. I know first I'll have to build us a house. Good thing I have Jack and Charles as helpers!"

She laughed. "I'm not sure how much help they'll be, but I guarantee they'll try."

Elmer smiled, brushing a kiss onto the top of her head. "What kind of house do you want?" he asked.

"I have no idea how to answer that. I'll need a cellar to keep food fresh, of course. A kitchen to cook in. Maybe a parlor for guests. We'll want at least three bedrooms, but I think we'll want more than that. Jack and Charles will share, but Poppy will need a room of her own, and I'm sure we'll want a room of our own."

"Yes, we will!" Elmer said, agreeing with a bedroom for them.

"What about a dining room? I'd like a kitchen big enough that we can eat at a table in there, but a nice dining room with a longer table where we can eat with guests will be nice. We're going to know the whole settlement at first."

"I hope it doesn't get too crowded there. There's a lake not far from Clover Creek called Bear Lake. I hope the lake doesn't bring too many people because I have no desire to live in a large city."

"I think it'll be a few years before we have to worry about that," Sarah said, smiling. She felt the same way. She wanted a quiet life without saloons and brothels around them.

"I can't wait to see if I got the plot of land I thought I did. The map doesn't look anything like what we saw while we were there, but I'm sure we're going to be happy with whatever land we got."

Sarah yawned. "I'm starting to get sleepy. Today felt like a day off in some ways, but it also felt like a hard day of work. I should gather the children so they can get ready for bed."

When she went to stand, the arm he had around her held her in place. She looked at him, wondering why he was keeping her there.

In answer to the question on her face, he lowered his lips to hers, and kissed her the way he'd been wanting to kiss her since they'd left Independence. The kiss was soft, but it was also probing. She turned more fully toward him and wrapped her arms around his shoulders.

When he finally pulled away, she saw stars, which she thought was a perfectly silly thing to see. "I need to get the children."

He ran his thumb over her lips, even as he nodded. "Find the children."

Chapter Six

Saturday, August 21st, 1852

Being married is something else. Sarah rises early as I do, and we spend some quiet time together before the rest of the camp wakes. I watch her make breakfast and I write in my journal.

I enjoy getting to know her a little more each day. And her siblings are fun young people. I do enjoy that Jack has taken to following me around and helping me with whatever he can.

We're now headed back to Clover Creek where we were camped several weeks ago. We should be able to make it back by mid-September if the captains keep up the pace we've been moving at. They say by traveling twenty-five miles per day and taking no days off unless we hit severe rains, we'll have more time to get our homes finished by winter. I think this first year will be a log cabin, and next summer will be a real house. I can then use the cabin as my workshop.

I do not feel like we'll have time to build a house before winter, and I want my family to be safe and warm through our coldest season. I do not know what the cold temperatures will be like in Clover Creek, and I pray they aren't as bad as they are in Pennsylvania. At least I will have my family to help me chink while I build. I can put the children on it immediately while Sarah can help as she has time.

I know we can make it before winter. I'm determined. I have a family to take care of now, and it is my greatest desire to see them content.

Perhaps by winter, we'll have another addition to the family growing. I love the idea of having babies with Sarah. Hopefully it will happen soon.

Driving the following day, Elmer counted his blessings. He hadn't had to buy a wagon, which would have eaten up all his money. He had a family now. He had two claims waiting for him in Clover Creek. And he would have the tools he needed to begin the carpentry work he'd been training for.

There were even enough oxen that he could start a small ranch as well. He knew a lot of work went into ranching, but he had help. It would be glorious.

While Elmer dreamed of the future, Sarah trudged behind the wagons with her friends and all the children. Mary was walking around with her musket to her shoulder, trying to get some meat for their suppers. Hannah was beside Sarah because she was worried about her friend.

"I really think you should talk to Jed about your anger toward God. I'm not saying I wouldn't be angry in your shoes, but my Jed always has the right words in situations like this."

Sarah sighed. "I'm not ready. Perhaps in a week or two I'll be able to talk about all of it, but I lost my father just three days ago. I should be allowed to be mad for a while."

Hannah sighed. "I really do think Jed could make you feel better."

"Perhaps. I'll talk to him when I'm ready."

Katie Bedwell joined them then. "How are you holding up, Sarah? Losing your father and marrying the next day...that's a very bold move."

Sarah sighed. "I'm doing my best for the children."

"There is no doubt in my mind that's what you're doing," Katie said. "I know how frightened I was when my husband died, and how afraid I was to take on a new husband when I didn't know how the children would be treated. It's all worked out for me, though."

Sarah smiled. "I'm glad. I think it's going to work out for me too. The children seem happy, and I have a great deal of respect for Elmer."

"And from what I understand, marrying you when he did benefitted him as well." Katie looked behind her to check on the children. "Our group seems so much smaller with just two families gone."

"Think of who left though," Sarah said, shaking her head. "The two worst behaved boys in the company, and Edna Blue, who wasn't poorly behaved just…different."

"She certainly did make an impression, didn't she?" Hannah responded. "I wish all the families had settled with us, but I can understand why some needed to go their own way."

"Are we still doing our twenty-five-mile days without Sundays off?" Sarah asked.

"We are," Hannah said. "The captains want us to have time to build before winter, and we've made almost miraculous time the whole journey. We're going to make the most of it. The captain wants us back in Clover Creek by mid-September, so we have the best chance of making it through the winter."

"It's strange only having one captain again," Katie said. "But Mr. Cauldron and his family went a different way. I do hope we'll see them again."

"I do as well. They may feel the need to visit because Betty, Mrs. Cauldron's sister, is settling near us," Hannah said. "I'm so thankful we'll have a doctor in our settlement."

"Yes!" Sarah said. "I worry that without a doctor we'd end up like the Roanoke Colony."

"We'll have a blacksmith, many farmers, many ranchers, a general store, a restaurant, a boarding house, and so much more!"

"A furniture maker," Sarah added.

"Elmer?" Hannah asked.

Sarah nodded. "His father wanted him to farm with him, but Elmer has already been through an apprenticeship for furniture, and he won't change his mind."

"Is that the problem between the two of them?" Hannah asked, shaking her head. "Why do men have to be so hardheaded about everything?"

"Are you saying the pastor is something less than perfect?" Katie asked.

Hannah laughed. "Of course not. Oh, and we'll have a preacher. It will feel like a real town rather quickly."

"It will *be* a real town quickly," Sarah said. "Elmer wants to be outside of town. He wants a plot with more trees so he can use them to make his furniture."

"I hope he makes rocking chairs," Hannah said. "I'm going to want one when the baby comes."

"That would be wonderful, wouldn't it?" Katie asked. "I'm hoping I can talk George into making one for me before our little one makes an appearance."

"Are you expecting as well?" Sarah asked. At times it felt like she was the only woman in the company who hadn't gotten pregnant along the trail.

Katie nodded. "It happened very quickly. I wasn't expecting to have more children, but I won't turn down a blessing from God."

Sarah smiled. "I'm sure it will be a beautiful baby." She said nothing about the blessing from God part of things. Why would he be blessing others and taking people from her? What had she done that was so terrible she deserved to have her parents killed?

For the noon meal, they had leftovers from the night before. Elmer prayed, blessing the hands who had prepared the food. "I had no idea I was marrying such a good cook."

Sarah smiled. "I enjoy cooking. I'm glad you like it. I have a feeling you'll be eating a lot of my cooking in the future."

"I think you're probably right about that." He grinned at her.

Poppy ate her food, but said, "Mother used to make us chicken and dumplings. Will you make me chicken and dumplings, Sarah?"

"Well, it's hard to make them on the trail, but once we settle in Clover Creek, I'll make them for you. I like them too." Sarah smiled at her sister, who seemed content with knowing she would get chicken and dumplings soon.

"How long until we reach Clover Creek?"

"A month or so."

"A month! We've already been walking for fifteen years!"

Sarah laughed. "How is that possible when you were already five when we started, and now you're six?"

"I don't know!" Poppy stamped her foot. "I don't want to walk anymore!"

To Sarah's surprise, Elmer said, "You are always welcome to sit on the wagon seat with me. You don't have to do it all day, but it would give your little feet a break from walking so much."

Poppy looked down at her feet. "My feet aren't little! They're big!"

Elmer chuckled. "Pardon me. They are much bigger than I realized."

Poppy wandered away then, not seeming to care about riding in the wagon.

Sarah smiled at Elmer. "I think you handled her perfectly. You gave her a choice about walking, and now she knows she can do what she wants. I think all of us just need choices."

"We have four more hours to go this afternoon. You can ride with me as well."

Sarah smiled, realizing she was thinking more highly of this man than she thought she would be. "I'm glad I married you, Elmer."

A smile lit up his face. "That's awfully nice to hear!"

"You're a good person, and I would have to be crazy not to be pleased," she said softly.

The day was long, and they walked until almost sunset as always. When they reached their destination for the day—the same spot where they'd camped the night her father had died—Sarah sat looking at the trail sadly. There was no remnant of his grave as they had driven every wagon over the spot where they'd buried him.

Sarah remembered exactly where he'd been buried and returned to the spot, kneeling beside his grave. "I'm sorry you died, Father, but I think we're going to be all right." She took a deep breath, realizing it was a privilege to be able to visit his grave one last time. She'd never been able to return to her mother's. "I married the King boy, Elmer. He's agreed to help me raise the children, and I think I'm falling in love with him. We all miss you so much, but we're going to go on without you because there's nothing else we can do."

Elmer found her there ten minutes later, the tears still streaming down her face. "Are you all right?" he asked, kneeling on the ground beside her.

She sniffled and nodded. "This was where we buried my father. You can't even see that it was once a grave."

His arm went around her, and he pulled her against him. "I'm so sorry."

"Me too." She let herself rest against him for a moment, and then got to her feet. "Supper needs to be fixed, and I do believe this is a good place to do laundry."

"There's dancing tonight," he said softly. "I'd love to dance with you."

She smiled and nodded. "I'll do the laundry, and while it's drying, we'll dance. Poppy will help me. She won't like it, but she'll do it."

"What's for supper?" he asked.

She smiled. "I thought I'd take some jerky and cut it into tiny pieces, then make a gravy from it that I'll serve over mashed potatoes. I'm so glad they had potatoes in stock."

"That sounds delicious. My ma wanted to make something like that, and my pa said he wouldn't eat it. We had beans any night there wasn't fresh meat, so almost every single night." He shook his head. "Save a few of the potatoes, and we'll plant them in the spring. I don't know if they'll grow, but I certainly do hope so!"

"I'm a little more adventurous of a cook than that. You may find yourself eating some very strange things being married to me."

He laughed. "Sounds like I'll have a lifetime of adventure with you."

She giggled a little. "I think you may." Having gone to her father's grave, and telling him how she was handling things, lifted her heart. She found it easy to laugh now. She'd visit once more before they left in the morning, but she didn't think it would be as hard as it had been the last time.

When they reached the wagon, she climbed in for the potatoes, flour, and jerky. Taking them all near the fire, she set everything down, and then she got some water that had already been boiled.

Elmer watched her cook as if it was the most fascinating thing he'd ever seen. While he watched, he held a knife in one hand and a wooden block in the other. When it was time to eat, he tucked the block into his pocket.

"What were you making?" she asked.

He shrugged. "Nothing much."

As soon as supper was over, Sarah had the children gather their dirty things and get dressed up for the dance. She decided to take Hannah's advice that evening and wear her blue dress, but she wouldn't change until the laundry was done.

At the river, there were several other women there doing the same as she was.

Poppy helped by handing her each item of clothing and she scrubbed it quickly in the river. Doing laundry on the trail was much quicker than at home, because they didn't have much time. They didn't boil water, and they only used soap and scrubbed on rocks, rinsed, and hung it to dry. The half-day process became just an hour.

As she finished rinsing and wringing out the last thing, she heard the musicians, and she smiled, knowing she'd be dancing with Elmer for the first time.

As she and Poppy walked back to camp, she talked about how much fun the dance would be.

Poppy frowned. "But Jimmy and Johnny aren't here anymore."

"And you like dancing with them?"

"Yes!"

"I'm sure that either one of your brothers would be happy to dance with you. Just ask them." Sarah really didn't understand the problem.

Poppy made a face. "They both stink. I don't want to get too close to them."

"They stink?" Sarah asked. "I'll make them take a bath in the river tonight."

"Can I take a bath in the river too?" Poppy asked.

"No, girls don't bathe in the river."

"I'm sick of being a girl. Can I be a boy?"

"It's just not that simple. Now run along to the dance. I'll be there after I hang the clothes." Sarah tied a string from her wagon to the one beside it and hung all her laundry there. Then she found Hannah, who happily held up a blanket for her so she could change in privacy—she was shielded on both sides by wagons, to her front by the laundry hanging, and to the rear by Hannah.

When she was ready, she looked at Hannah. "I think I'm ready."

Hannah smiled. "I know you are!"

Chapter Seven

Saturday August 21st, 1852

We are once again camped where my father died. It seems strange to be here, but I had the opportunity to sit at his grave and talk to him about what has transpired since his demise. I need to remember that he and Mother are together again, and probably dancing across all the clouds together, but...it's not that simple. My parents were not old people when they died, and they were both in good health. Why has God taken them from us?

Tonight is the first night I will participate in the dancing that happens in camp every Saturday night. I am looking forward to dancing with my Elmer, and he has made it clear that he wants me to dance with him. I think I'm developing feelings for him. He is a good man, which I was told over and over, but he's gentle and good with the children. I almost wonder if I deserve a man like him, with my questioning God at every turn.

I do hope the dancing will still be fun to watch, even without Edna Blue to spin the night away and bump into people. Of course, there's always Bob and Mary, who do some demented form of wiggling around and call it dancing. They tend to crash into at least four other couples on any given night.

SARAH'S SIBLINGS

I never went to a dance at home, but now I dream about going to dances there in Clover Creek. I will spend my evenings in the arms of Elmer, the man I love.

Wait...love? Dare I say that? I've only really known him for a few days, and love doesn't come on that quickly. My mother once told me she didn't love my father until her third child was born. It took her that long to develop feelings with a man who she had pledged her life to. No, it can't be love yet. He just makes me feel comforted, and that's why that word popped into my mind.

Maybe someday I will fall in love with him with his sweet smile and hard-working ways, but I cannot guarantee it will happen.

Putting her journal down, Sarah arrived at the dance late, but she immediately spotted her husband sitting with her siblings. Mary and Bob were on the dance floor, and sure enough, Mary had to keep apologizing to the people around them.

Sarah was shaking her head as she sat down. Elmer looked toward her. "Are you telling me you won't dance with me?"

"Of course not. You're my husband. Who else would I dance with?" Sarah sat beside Poppy and realized all three children were between her and Elmer.

"The next song?" he asked.

Sarah nodded to the dance floor. "Watch Bob and Mary for a minute. They bump into everyone else at least four times per night. It might be best if we waited until they sit a song out before we attempt to dance."

Elmer sat and watched Bob and Mary, laughing as he did. "I think we'll be okay. I'll make sure my back is always to them to protect you."

"Are you sure?" Sarah asked. "You haven't seen the utter mayhem they cause. Between those two and Edna Blue, it was a game to see how many dancers they could each injure. Well, not really but it looked like it."

"We'll beat them at their own game!" he said, taking her hand and helping her to her feet.

"We're not going to run people over like they are!" she protested.

"No, but we're not going to let them run us over either." Elmer led her to the "dancefloor" and pulled her into his arms.

The song was a slow one, but that didn't stop Bob and Mary from doing a wild dance that was going to take someone's eye out. Sarah had never seen a couple as suited to one another as Bob and Mary were. Even their dance styles—if they could be called that—were similar.

True to his word, Elmer kept his back to Bob and Mary, and when they bumped into him, he brought his elbow back, not too hard, but it hit Bob square in his side.

"Hey!" Bob said. "You can't do that on a dancefloor."

"You bump into me, and I bump into you."

Elmer knew Bob wouldn't confront him, so he held his ground.

Bob sighed. "I think we need to stay on the other side of the dancefloor tonight. Elmer thinks he's the king of the dance. King Elmer? No, King Bob sounds so much better!"

Mary smiled. "King Bob and Queen Mary. I'll remind Sarah of the real power couple here tomorrow."

As they walked to the other end of the dancefloor, Sarah couldn't help but laugh. "I can't believe they're going to leave us alone!"

When others saw that Sarah and Elmer were alone on one side of the dancefloor, they were slowly joined by other couples. First, Hannah and Jed, and then Margaret and Jamie. Both women were pregnant, and it wouldn't have been safe to dance near Bob and Mary.

After Bob and Mary went to the other side of the dancefloor, Sarah let herself sink into Elmer and truly enjoy dancing with him. Being held in his arms was the most wonderful thing she could ever remember experiencing.

She rested her head on his shoulder and sighed contentedly. Elmer had become her rock in a matter of days. She felt safe with him, and it was a new feeling.

It was six songs later when they left the dancefloor, going back to sit with her siblings. Poppy looked at Sarah. "You danced for a long time. It's my turn to dance with Elmer."

Elmer looked surprised but only for a moment. He held his hand out and Poppy took it, holding her head up high.

Once on the dancefloor, Poppy stood on Elmer's feet and he danced her around, smiling down at her happy little face. He truly felt as if he belonged in this new family of his, and that surprised him.

Sarah wasn't even surprised by the tear that sprang to her eye. Her father had never interacted with his children the way Elmer was with Poppy. He'd been a good father and a good provider, but it never would have occurred to him to dance with Poppy the way Elmer was. Or in any way for that matter. He thought his role as a father began and ended with making a living. Sarah wouldn't have ever thought to want to dance with her father.

But now...she could only think of how a real opportunity had been missed and it was now much too late to do anything about it.

Elmer and Sarah spent as much time on the dancefloor that evening as they did off it. Sarah felt closer to Elmer than she had, and she realized that he was a man she could fall in love with, much faster than after fifteen years of marriage too. Her parents had never been demonstrative, and Sarah assumed that they were affectionate behind closed doors, but now she wondered. Had her parents just never craved affection from one another? Whatever reason, she felt sad for them.

That evening after the dance, Sarah made sure the children were bedded down before putting a blanket over her shoulder and taking Elmer's hand, leading him away from the camp. She knew she didn't have to do anything for a few days yet, but she needed Elmer to see how she felt about him. How much affection she had for him, and even her blossoming love. Maybe she couldn't say it yet, but she had a feeling showing him would make him just as happy.

Once they were away from the others, she spread the blanket on the ground, and Elmer looked at her curiously. "Are you trying to tell me something?" he asked.

Instead of answering, Sarah walked into his arms and rose up on her tiptoes to kiss him. Elmer didn't need any more prompting than that. His hands ran all over her body, and he slowly undressed them both.

He wished he could see her, but it was just a quarter moon, and despite how bright the stars seemed, they didn't light her enough. He was certain it was all right though because he would touch every inch of her and learn her body that way.

When they finally laid down on the blanket and became one, Sarah wondered how she could have refused Elmer on that first night. She enjoyed what they were doing together, but she could tell he enjoyed it a great deal more than she did.

Afterward, he held her close and covered her face with kisses. "Thank you."

Sarah grinned. Only Elmer would think to thank her after they consummated their marriage. "Oh, no thanks necessary. We should try this again and again."

He chuckled. "Exactly what I was thinking. I wish we didn't have to sneak off into the night as if we were doing something wrong, but I'm sure it will be better in Clover Creek, when we have a house with a door on the bedroom."

"You make a good point!" she said.

On their walk back to their wagon, they passed Bob and Mary who were headed out for some private time of their own judging by the blanket tucked under Mary's arm.

"Should we pretend we don't see them?" Sarah whispered.

Elmer laughed softly. "If we pretend we don't see them, they'll pretend they don't see us. It's probably for the best if we don't think about what they're doing out here."

Sarah didn't argue with him. She was sure he was right. She was just glad she had never seen her parents sneaking out onto the prairie. Never had it occurred to her why the young couples were always leaving camp while everyone else was sleeping, but now she understood completely. They wanted to love one another just as she and Elmer just had.

When they got back to camp, instead of crawling into their tent with Poppy, Sarah spread their blanket out and grabbed another from under the wagon to cover them. Maybe they wouldn't have privacy, but what could be more romantic than sleeping under the stars with her new husband?

When Sarah woke in the morning, she realized she was snuggled up against Elmer. Thankfully, it wasn't dawn yet, so no one would have seen them.

As she extricated herself from Elmer's embrace, he woke and wrapped his arms around her. "I like being able to hold you, wife."

"I need to put our breakfast on. You can sleep for a little longer."

Instead, Elmer got up and they folded their blankets together, putting them into the back of the wagon. Elmer took the small block of wood he'd been working with, and he pulled out a knife.

While Sarah cooked, Elmer carved. "What are you making?"

"No idea," he said, but his hand shielded his project from her.

Sarah frowned. "Are you lying to me this early in our marriage?" she asked.

"Not at all. I'm simply being evasive. See the difference?"

She laughed. "I guess I do. I'm making johnny cakes for the children again," she said, holding a mixing bowl against her stomach with one hand and using the other to stir the mixture. "If you want anything else, I'm happy to make it."

"I'm not going to ask you to make two breakfasts. Besides, I've discovered I love johnny cakes."

"You have good taste," she said, smiling at him.

"Of course, I do," he responded. "Look who I married."

"Thank you for dancing with Poppy last night," she said softly. "Father never spent time with any of us that way, and it looked so sweet. I know Poppy really enjoyed it."

"My father never did anything like that either," he said, "but Ma always tried to find fun in everything we did. I remember dancing with her in the kitchen to an old music box."

"That sounds like a perfectly lovely time," she said, smiling at the thought. "I should make certain to do that with my brothers."

"Do it soon. As soon as I was thirteen, I was done dancing with Ma."

"And then who did you dance with?" She found that she was a little jealous of any girl he'd courted before her.

"No one. I went to be an apprentice at sixteen, and all the time I wasn't helping my father on the farm, I was making furniture."

"At least you weren't out on the streets getting into trouble."

He chuckled. "All of my close neighbors were Amish. The Amish boys had no desire to get into trouble, so I was on my own. Ma taught me to read and write and do math. I never learned much of anything else. Other than crafting furniture of course."

"Well, I wouldn't guess Amish boys would be inclined to trouble the way other boys are. Just don't teach my brothers to get into trouble please." She carefully flipped the johnny cakes onto five plates, handing Elmer's to him. "I should have had you wake the children while I cooked. I never even thought of that."

"I'll remember tomorrow morning to wake them." He yawned. "I miss taking Sundays off each week."

"I do too." She wouldn't miss the church service though. They'd taken to having them after walking all day on Sunday, and she would claim to be too tired. There was no way she was going to sit with other people to worship a God who had forsaken her.

"You're welcome to ride with me anytime. I know the children are capable of caring for themselves for a few hours," Elmer said, waiting to eat until the children were awake.

As soon as they were all gathered around the fire, he thanked God for the food and his new family. He couldn't believe how much he was enjoying being a father-figure to her siblings. He genuinely cared for the children. Not like he cared for Sarah, of course, but he enjoyed being around them.

After complimenting Sarah on their breakfast, he looked at Jack. "Let's make sure we get a different pair of oxen today. Did your father have a rotation plan for them?"

Jack shook his head. "He just chose whichever two looked fresh. Now, I don't know what it means for an ox to look fresh, but Father always seemed to know which ones to choose."

"Well, I'll see if I can point out the fresh ones then."

"If you figure it out, you need to teach me. Are we going to have a ranch in Clover Creek like Father wanted?"

Elmer thought about it for a moment. "Do you feel like it would honor your father to have a ranch?"

Jack nodded. "I do."

"It won't be a big ranch, but we'll have a ranch. Does that work?"

The smile on Jack's face was answer enough for all of them.

Chapter Eight

Sunday, August 22nd, 1852

My beautiful wife did not make me wait a full week. I'm enjoying the children more than I can say, so when Poppy, Sarah's youngest sibling, asked me to dance last night, I complied. She stood on my feet as we danced around.

I much preferred dancing with my Sarah as anyone would expect, but I made sure to dance with Poppy enough that she felt as if she was my date as well. I told Sarah how my ma would dance with me in the kitchen to the tune of an old music box she had. Her parents weren't playful with her and her siblings, so she is going to try to dance with her brothers in the kitchen.

This morning at breakfast, Jack, the older boy, asked if we were going to ranch like his father had planned. They were moving west to ranch, and they have more than enough oxen to start that ranch. I've decided that I will run a small ranch to honor him. I have a feeling one of the boys will want to make a living ranching, and I will pave the way for him to do that. It's only right.

We're moving twenty-five miles again today. We'll have our church service after our day of travel, though. I know the church service will bring comfort to Sarah. She's gone to the service every week we've been on the trail. I will feel so proud to sit beside her and worship with her and her brothers and sister. I know that feels strange, but my Sarah is everything to me. If she wanted to ranch, I would give up all ideas of carpentry work, but only for her. I can't do it for my pa.

Thankfully, she seems content with the idea of me making furniture, and she's even agreed to helping in whatever way she can. I would like to see one of the boys learn the trade, but if they would both be happier ranching, so be it. Maybe one of the sons Sarah and I have together would enjoy furniture making. I do believe it's the only trade truly suited to me.

After their long day of travel, Sarah made a meal of beans with rice. Her siblings didn't complain because the last time they had, she told them she would happily throw it out, but she would never again cook anything for them.

As they ate their supper, Elmer suggested just wearing their everyday clothes for church. "God understands how hard this journey is on all of us, and he'll understand if we don't dress for worship."

Sarah took a deep breath, her mind whirling. She had no intention of going to the service that evening. She may never even go again. "I'm not sure I'm going to the service tonight. Why don't you take the children?"

Elmer looked at her, confused. "Are you not feeling well?" he asked.

"I'm fine. I was thinking of starting some bread while you are there, and I'll bake it before we go to sleep. I want to make the most of my time." Sarah couldn't force her eyes to meet his as she fibbed. She'd tell him later. Just not in front of the children.

While Elmer and her siblings were at the church service, Sarah pounded out her frustration with God on a defenseless loaf of bread. She could hear the singing from across the camp, down by the river, but she wasn't about to be part of it.

She put the bread dough into a bowl, and set it aside, covering the bowl with a clean cloth as her mother had taught her. She wasn't even certain why she did it, but she knew it was the way it was done.

She looked all around her at the beauty of the earth, and she knew deep within her that God had to be real. Nothing so truly awesome could happen by chance. If only she could get past her anger, all would be good again. She wasn't sure one could call herself a Christian if she didn't attend church services, but she felt closer to God sitting there in nature, admiring his handiwork.

A shadow fell across the campfire, and Sarah looked up to see Hannah. "Why aren't you at the service?" Sarah asked. "Are you sick?"

"No, I'm not sick. But my dear friend is hurting, and I'm not going to leave her sitting alone, baking bread as an excuse to get out of service." Hannah sat down on the ground beside Sarah. "Talk to me about it."

"You don't want me to spew my vitriol. I'm furious with God. You're a preacher's wife. You shouldn't have to listen to me."

"I want to listen to you, Sarah. I really do. Tell me what's going through your mind."

"We started on this journey west because my father wanted to own a large ranch. With the free government land, he would have enough land to do what he wanted to do. We sold everything we owned. Everything. We only kept our clothing, and Mother kept her jewelry, music box, and her family Bible."

Hannah nodded. Most of the company had similar stories.

"I had the choice of joining my family and moving west or staying and finding a job to support myself. I knew how treacherous the journey would be, so I decided to go along, to make the trek easier for my mother." Sarah took a deep breath. "When Mother died just a couple of weeks into our journey, I cried, and I mourned her, but I knew it would all be fine, because I could do the laundry, the cooking, and mind the children, while Father drove the wagon and took care of the oxen he'd brought with us, which he wanted to use to start his beef herd."

"Yes, I can see your reasoning there." Hannah looked at her expectantly, wanting to hear more of the story.

"We did well, with my father, the three children, and me. I don't mind hard work, and I pitched in and took over my mother's chores." Sarah hugged her knees to her chest. "Then we made it to Clover Creek, and Father and I were both excited that it was the place chosen by the whole company. It was where we wanted to settle."

Hannah smiled. "I still see Clover Creek in my dreams."

Sarah sighed. "But Father died two days before we reached Oregon City. He's talked to me about Oregon City so many times, I thought my head would explode. But he was happy with the idea of starting his ranch. Why couldn't he have at least made it to Oregon City? Why did he have to die then? Would two more days have been too much to ask?"

"Do you remember how your father died, Sarah?"

"Of course, he fell out of his seat dead."

"But what led to that?"

Sarah sighed. "He wouldn't drink cold coffee all day and kept drinking water straight from the rivers."

"Exactly. We know that we need to boil water. We don't know why, but we know it keeps people alive on the trail. That's why we all feed coffee and tea to babies barely old enough to toddle. So that they will stay safe." Hannah shook her head. "He knew as we all did, he needed to only drink tea or coffee. Instead of listening to the doctor or anyone else about it, he drank unsafe water. Does that make it God's fault that he died?"

"Don't try to reason with me while I'm busy being angry at God!" Sarah said, but she knew deep down her friend was right. Was it good her father had been taken from her before they reached Oregon City? Of course not. Was it her father's fault or God's? She knew the answer to that as well. Even though she didn't want to admit it, she knew God had nothing to do with taking her father.

"I'm going back to the service now, but I want you to think about what I said. You can rage at God all you want, but it won't bring your father back, and it won't be God's fault it happened." Hannah stood and walked away, while Sarah sat on the ground, wanting to stay angry with God, but knowing she really couldn't.

She took the dough and punched it down, kneading it a little more as she'd been taught. As she worked the dough this time, she was angry with her father, realizing the blame should be on him and not on God. Why hadn't he agreed to drink the cold coffee she and her siblings drank all day? She'd even served them all coffee instead of tea to please him.

Finally, she put the dough in a baking pan, then added green sticks into her Dutch oven and put the baking pan in as well, atop green sticks. Then she covered it all with a cloth so it could rise once more. While she waited for the service to be over, she prayed, asking God to forgive her for being so angry with him.

When the family came back to the campfire, she and Elmer got the children into their makeshift beds, and Elmer looked at her, as if trying to figure something out. "Let's go for a walk."

Sarah nodded. "I'm going to put the bread on so it can cook while we walk and talk." She replaced the cloth with the lid of the Dutch oven and put the whole thing into the embers of the fire. She grabbed a blanket, just in case, and they walked away from camp.

"Why didn't you want to go to church tonight? I've never seen you miss a service." He was truly worried about her behavior. She usually seemed fine, but anytime church was mentioned, she'd seem to shy away.

"I have been angry with God since my father died. I should have said something sooner. Hannah came to me during the service and showed me that I was wrong to blame God, and I am feeling a bit better, but now I'm angry with my father."

Elmer sighed. "What were you angry about?"

"My father's death. You see, I was blaming him for losing both of my parents on the trail. But Hannah reminded me that the only reason my father died is he kept drinking water out of the river, instead of drinking the coffee I made for him. I prefer tea, but I made coffee and drank it all day, so he could have his coffee. But he didn't like cold coffee and didn't want to drink any coffee other than the mornings, so he always drank from the rivers, and he died. I've prayed for forgiveness for being angry in the first place, and I'll be going to services again."

Elmer wrapped his arm around her shoulders. "I'm sorry you were so upset, and I wish you'd come to me."

Sarah nodded. "That's exactly what I should have done, but I felt like it was my problem, not someone else's."

"But you told Hannah..."

"Hannah mostly figured it out. She's a smart woman, you know."

"I'm sure she is." He stopped walking and put his arms around her, kissing her softly. "Are you feeling better now, or should we just go back to camp?"

Sarah smiled. "I do feel better. Maybe we should take a longer walk."

"Will the bread burn?"

"It won't."

He took the blanket from her and spread it out, and before she knew what was happening, he was removing her dress.

When they returned to camp, Sarah checked the bread and smiled. "That was a good way for us to time the baking bread," she said, smiling at Elmer. She knew she should be a little shyer around him, but she wasn't exactly certain as to why. She decided to not pretend and just be herself.

As they settled onto the ground the same way they had the previous night, Elmer talked to her some more about her feelings. "I believe I'd be angry as well. Do the children know why you didn't go?"

Sarah turned onto her side, so she was facing her husband. "They don't, and I'd rather they didn't. They don't need to know that their big sister had a meltdown when their father died. It would be harder for them to respect me."

"If that's how you want it to be, then that's exactly how it will be. I won't tell them anything you don't think they should know. Ever. I believe that should always be your choice." He stroked her cheek with one finger. "I think many of the things about raising them should be decided together, but that's one thing that you can choose on your own."

"Thank you." Sarah scooted more toward him so they could sleep close to one another. "If there's anything we need to discuss that's not related to my irrational feelings, then I'm happy to talk about it whenever you're ready."

"I do have a question."

"What?"

"I want to know how many bedrooms you think the cabin needs. I mean, we need at least one so we can have privacy for our married adventures, but do we need two more? It'll only be for the winter."

"I think one is enough. The children can sleep on the floor. They're quite used to not using beds now."

"I will build us a bed, but I think we may be on the floor this first year as well."

"I guessed as much. You'll have time to build a cabin or time to make furniture. I'll take the cabin first, and the furniture later. It would be nice to have a table and chairs when you can make them work." Before they'd left Independence, she didn't think she'd have ever said that it didn't matter if she slept in a bed or not, but life on the trail had taught Sarah many things, one of the most important had been that her comfort wasn't the most important thing in the world.

"Then we'll wait with a bed until we build the new house. Why don't I make a table and two benches? We can all sit and eat together, but it will be much quicker. I'm going to need to build a fireplace, and you'll be cooking over that the first year. I hope that's all right. Everything else will come in time."

Sarah nodded. "That sounds perfect. I'm glad in a way that you're willing to run a small ranch. The boys have cattle ranches romanticized in their heads because of how long Father was telling them we needed one."

"If you wanted me to just ranch, I would do it happily. I'd rather make furniture, but it doesn't matter too much to me." Elmer kissed the top of her head.

"Thank you for that. But no, a small ranch and you build your furniture shop."

He sighed as he wrapped his arms around her and settled in for the night. He was much happier having Sarah to hold all night long.

Chapter Nine

Monday, August 23rd, 1852

I didn't go to our church service last night because I was too angry with God to go. During the service Hannah had a talk with me and made me realize that my father chose to do things that he knew could cost him his life. For a while, I redirected my anger at Father, but now I'm much calmer. Perhaps he felt the need to be with Mother? As much as I didn't notice affection between them, they were married for more than twenty years, and I know there must have been some there.

I feel content about the situation now, and I'm very quickly falling in love with my Elmer. It doesn't matter to me if it took my mother more than fifteen years to fall in love. I can do things my own way, and my way is to choose to love my husband every day for the rest of my life.

We are camped along the Columbia River, and I'm excited that we are headed back to our forever home in Clover Creek. With water at the ready and wood to be chopped, it will be a perfect place for all of us to settle. We'll have a doctor and a preacher and even a blacksmith. Whatever we need we'll be able to take care of right there in town.

Elmer and I have talked of a cabin for the first winter, because there will be very little time to build before the snows come. But he will build us a real house next summer with at least four bedrooms, a kitchen, parlor, and a dining room. And a cellar. I'll have a cellar to store food. Oh, it all sounds like a dream come true. Granted, it will be another year, but I can live in that cabin for as long as I need to. I've been living out of a wagon for five months. What's a year in a cabin?

Elmer has agreed to start a small ranch that one of the boys can take over when they are ready. I know he would like one of the boys to follow in his own footsteps, but he is honoring my father by starting a ranch.

I just want a small homestead. I want to be able to plant a kitchen garden every year and breed the cattle. It would be nice to have a few chickens as well. Whatever happens I know it will be good because Elmer will make sure it is.

Sarah made a point of walking with Mrs. King on Monday morning. "Thank you for what you told me about Elmer. He's such a good man, and I don't know if I would have seen it without your advice."

Mrs. King smiled. "He is. Whether he and his father see eye-to-eye or not, they're both good men." She seemed pleased to hear that Sarah agreed her son was a good man.

"I sure hope our claims will be close to one another. My siblings could use grandparents, as well as the children Elmer and I will have together." Sarah wasn't sure how the older woman would feel about being a grandparent to a child that wasn't blood related, but Mrs. King surprised her.

"Oh, thank you! I wanted a houseful of children, but God only gave me one. I would like at least twelve grandchildren."

Sarah smiled. "If I can carry them, I will have them." She had no qualms about having a large family. It simply seemed right to her. "And now that my parents are gone, I would love the children to have a wonderful grandmother like you."

Mrs. King's eyes filled with tears. "Would your family like to join ours for supper tonight?" she asked. "I would love to get to know my three grandchildren."

Sarah nodded. "Would you like me to come early so I can help make it?"

"Don't think I'm going to let you take the joy of cooking for my grandchildren from me." Mrs. King tried to sound as if she was scolding Sarah, but it didn't work out well.

"I made a large, strangely shaped loaf of bread last night. I could bring that to complement whatever it is you make."

Mrs. King nodded. "That would be wonderful. I believe I shall make something my husband will hate but that the children will enjoy. He's going to be pleased to have the children there."

"With having just lost their father, they may be a bit standoffish for a while, but they've warmed up to Elmer for certain." Sarah was glad she and her mother-in-law were of a like mind. And she realized that it wouldn't be just her and Elmer raising the children. It would be his parents as well.

"I don't think that will matter one bit to us," Mrs. King said. "If one of your brothers or one of your sons is interested in learning about farming, I promise you that my Isaiah would be the best teacher they could ask for."

Sarah nodded. "Elmer told me to save a few of the potatoes I purchased in Oregon City, so I can plant them in the spring. Maybe we'll have a potato farm!"

Mrs. King laughed. "I really don't think there will be a farm. Not if my Elmer has anything to say about it."

Sarah nodded her agreement. "That's true, but he agreed to start a small ranch for one of my brothers to take over, because that was my father's dream."

"That boy of mine really is a good man, isn't he?"

"He is."

After a while, Sarah went to sit on the wagon seat with Elmer. She had to give him a warning about them eating with his parents that night.

Elmer looked at her, and a smile spread across his face. "I sure do like it when you're close to me," he said. He put his arm around her shoulders and drew her closer.

"I feel exactly the same way," Sarah told him. "I'm here for a reason though."

"What's that?" he asked, coaxing the oxen to go a bit to the left of the trail because of a hole.

"I accepted a supper invitation from your mother. We're all going to be eating with your parents, and your mother said she'd fix something your father would hate but the children would love."

He stared straight ahead for a long moment before nodding. "I think it will be good if my parents can get to know you and your brothers and sister."

"I told your ma that she and your father would have to act as grandparents to my siblings, and she seemed overjoyed with the idea. And she wants us to have twelve children."

He smiled at that. "That doesn't surprise me even a little bit. She's the kind of mother who had a snack waiting for me every day when I came home from my apprenticeship, and she always made sure it was something Pa didn't like, so there was no chance he would eat it before I got there."

Sarah laughed softly. "Sounds like the perfect mother."

"Oh, she had her flaws, but I truly can't imagine a mother who would be better than her." Elmer's face was relaxed as he said the words, and Sarah knew he really thought a great deal of his mother.

"I'm glad you don't mind that I accepted. I went out of my way to walk with your mother this morning, so I could get to know her better. They're the only relatives we have left."

He slid his arm around her shoulders. "I promise I will make the next year of your life much better than the last has been. I'll do better every year, until things are so good, you don't remember anything bad ever happening to you."

Sarah smiled. "I'll make you keep that promise."

"You won't need to make me." He kissed her cheek and stroked her hair. "How did I ever deserve a wife like you?"

She chuckled. "You're the one who is special. Not me." She glanced at the terrain for the next bit before jumping down to walk some more. She liked being able to climb on the wagon seat and talk to him for a while, but the way the wagon shook her was downright painful. She wasn't going to ride any more than she absolutely needed to.

As she walked back toward the other women, Poppy hurried toward her. "Sarah, I want to ride with Elmer. He told me I could."

"Then let's go put you on the wagon with Elmer." Sarah took her sister's hand, hurrying back to where their wagon was in line, and helped her onto the wagon seat. "Have fun riding." With a grin at Elmer, she walked back toward the other women. Once she had, she wondered why she hadn't just stayed where she was. It would have been so much easier than doubling up on part of the walk. Of course, she was used to walking, and it didn't hurt her.

The rest of the day flew by as she thought about going to supper with the Kings. She had no idea what Mr. King was like, never having really spoken to him, but she was determined to like him. He may have had issue with her husband's chosen profession, but she was certain he was a good man. How else could Elmer have come from him?

After finishing up their daily walk, Sarah felt as if she didn't have any work to do, which was silly. A woman's work was never done, her mother used to say, and Sarah had realized how true her mother's words were.

She dug in the back of their wagon, and pulled out her mending basket, getting to work on clothes her brothers had ripped along the way. Mending was her least favorite task, and she tended to put it aside just as long as she could.

When Elmer got to camp after taking care of the oxen, Jack trailing along behind him, she smiled at her husband. "Do you have any mending that needs to be done?" she asked. "Since I don't have to cook tonight, I'm working on our mending, but realized I didn't have yours yet."

He frowned. "My mending is probably still in my mother's basket. She won't mind doing it and bringing it back to me," he said.

"I feel like I'm shirking my duties. I'll ask her about it this evening."

He sat beside her on the ground, moving one hand to the nape of her neck, under her hair. "You're the best wife a man could ask for." His kiss made her toes curl. "Feel like going for a walk later?"

She nodded. "I would love to go for a walk with you." Her body tingled as she thought about what the walk would entail. She'd never imagined she would enjoy making love with her husband, but every time, it was beautiful and special.

"See? The best wife a man could ask for."

At supper time, they gathered the children from the different places they were playing and walked to his parents' wagon. Sarah was all smiles. "I realized I haven't gotten Elmer's mending from you. From what I understand, one of the biggest joys of having a son marry, is you no longer have to mend his clothes."

Mrs. King laughed. "I have always enjoyed mending my men's clothes. You should bring me your mending as I can see you don't enjoy it. It would be my pleasure to help you with the task." She laughed. "Introduce me to these children of yours!"

Sarah smiled, pointing to each of her siblings proudly. "This is Jack, he's eight. This one is Charles, he's seven. And the little girl is Poppy, who is six. Children, this is Elmer's mother, so she's your new grandmother."

None of the children even questioned her words. Sarah knew Jack was old enough to know better, but he'd lost too much family to quibble. "Can we call you Grandma?" Jack asked.

Mrs. King nodded, and Sarah could see the tears brimming in her eyes. "I would be very happy if you called me Grandma."

Mr. King came into the camp then, looking confused to see Elmer and his new family. He looked into the pot, which held a mixture of sliced potatoes, what looked like chopped up jerky, and gravy. "I don't want to eat this," he said grumpily.

Mrs. King shot him a look that told him his words were unacceptable. "I thought it would be nice to serve something other than beans for our new grandchildren's first meal with us."

Mr. King looked stunned for a moment, before asking, "Are either of you boys interested in farming?"

To Sarah's surprise, Charles nodded. "Father wanted us to be ranchers, but I always liked the idea of having a farm one day. It would be fun to see what would grow."

A smile transformed Mr. King's face, and he no longer looked like a grumpy old man to Sarah. He looked a lot like Elmer in that moment. "What's your name, boy?"

"Charles, but you may call me Charlie."

"I'd like that. You may call me Granddad. I'm too young to be a grandpa."

Charles walked over to stand beside Mr. King, where he was sitting on the ground, waiting for his meal. "Will you teach me to farm, Granddad?"

"I would be the happiest man alive if you let me teach you to farm."

Sarah's gaze met Elmer's over the top of Poppy's head. He was smiling. "Now that I've found you a grandson who wants to farm, will you forgive me?"

SARAH'S SIBLINGS

The smile on Mr. King's face was the only answer any of them needed. He was thrilled to teach a boy to be a farmer. Especially when he could call the boy his grandson.

When Sarah looked over at Mrs. King, she could see tears in the older woman's eyes again. "What can I teach you, Poppy?" Mrs. King asked.

"I want to learn to make rag dolls," Poppy said. "My favorite doll fell in the river a long time ago, and I want another."

"I will teach you to make them then. I love to sew. Would you let me make you a dress?"

Poppy looked at Sarah to see if it was all right, and Sarah nodded. "Yes, please. I like yellow and blue best."

"Maybe we'll make your rag doll a dress that matches yours," Mrs. King suggested as she started serving each of them a bowl of food.

As they all sat on the ground for their meal, Mr. King said a prayer, thanking God for his new family. Sarah didn't need to hear the words he was saying to know how he felt. He was thrilled to have grandchildren, especially when one wanted to learn to farm.

Chapter Ten

Monday, August 30th, 1852

Thanks to Sarah, my relationship with my father has been restored. I don't know how she so easily accomplished something that had taken all the months on the trail to destroy.

When I first saw Sarah in Independence, I fell in love with her beauty, but I didn't know or care a great deal about what kind of personality she had. Now, I still see her beauty, of course, but it's her heart that has made me a captive. She never complains about being left with three children to feed and care for. She simply does her job as their new "mother."

I truly believe she is one of the most caring and beautiful women in all the west, and I am pleased that she is mine. My wife. My love. My everything.

It should not take much longer than three weeks for us to reach our destination in Clover Creek, and as soon as we arrive, we will start building shelter for the winter. I am thrilled that her brothers will help me, but even happier that my father and I will work together to accomplish the task.

He chose the plots beside my own, and we will be happy to have them as not only parents, but also as our closest neighbors. The idea of being able to go to Ma and Pa's for supper whenever we wish to makes me extremely happy. And Sarah and I can have them over as well.

All jobs are easier with two pairs of hands working on them, and that's what my father and I will do. We will work together to get our homes built. I will need to build a barn as well, I think. Maybe not a full barn, but enough for the oxen we have with us to shelter in through the winters. Pa doesn't plan on raising livestock. He wants to grow food, not be a dairyman.

If he keeps his oxen, they can use my shelter for the winter. Perhaps he will allow me to have them to help start our herd. Jack insists he wants to be a rancher, and I will help him work toward that goal. What better gift could I give him than a ranch that is already profitable?

After putting down his journal, Elmer looked at his wife just across the fire. His gift for her was almost complete, and he prayed she would like it. He'd worked on it almost every day since they'd married. He planned to give it to her during their walk that night.

As he watched, Sarah flipped the johnny cakes, and he took that as his cue to wake up the children. He woke the boys first, and despite their grumbles and eye-rubbing, they got up, going to find a place outside of camp to relieve themselves.

Then he ducked his head into Poppy's little tent, and when she saw who was waking her, her face lit up. "Elmer! Is it breakfast time?"

"It is. How's my sweet girl today?"

"Sleepy, but I can wake up if there are johnny cakes waiting for me," she said, rubbing her eyes.

"Your sister has them almost finished," he said in a whisper as if it was a big secret.

Poppy grinned, wrapped her arms around his neck, and gave him a loud, smacking kiss on the cheek. "I love you, Elmer."

The words surprised him, but also made him feel sad. He and Sarah hadn't said the words to one another yet. He felt them, but he didn't know how she felt. He knew then he would put his heart on the line that night during their walk and tell her how he felt. It was the right thing to do.

Poppy hurried out to join Elmer and Sarah for breakfast. "Where are the boys? Can we eat without them? I'm hungry!"

Sarah shook her head at her sister. "We can wait a few minutes for the boys to come back."

Poppy sighed dramatically. "I think I will probably *starve* to death!"

Elmer made a big show about taking one piece of bacon and handing it to her, while Sarah pretended not to see what happened. She was quite amused at the team Elmer and Poppy had formed. The little girl danced with him as often as she could talk him into it.

Sarah had danced with both of her younger brothers on Saturday night. Jack had seemed torn between letting himself enjoy the moment and wanting to pretend he didn't want to dance with her.

Sarah didn't care. She loved her brothers, and she was going to make their lives full of special moments, now that she knew she could. It was odd that she'd always accepted the way her parents raised her as the only way possible. Now she knew better, and she was going to make the most of it.

When the boys came back to camp, Sarah handed them each a plate before bowing her head for their morning prayer. Her feelings of anger—toward both God and her father—had dissipated. She missed her father horribly, but she no longer blamed him for causing his own death. What was the point? Her anger was only hurting her, not anyone else. So she chose to forgive, so she could have a happy life.

While they ate breakfast, they all talked about what they were going to do that day. "I'm walking forever," Poppy said. "But I think I may ride with Elmer too. He needs me to help him know the route."

Sarah smiled at that. The oxen just plodded along where there was a path, following the wagon in front of them. There wasn't much driving involved. In fact, some of the men led their oxen and didn't sit on the wagon seat to drive it. Usually, it depended on how much weight they had in their wagons. For larger families, it was harder to drive because there was only so much the oxen could pull.

The boys talked about how they were going to walk with some of the Mitchell boys. When they'd first left Independence the Mitchell boys had seemed like perfectly acceptable companions. They had, however, spent a great deal more time with the Cauldron boys than they should have, and now they got into a great deal of mischief. She'd seen Mary climb trees to get her brothers down more than once.

Of course, climbing trees was one of those things that Mary did that other young ladies weren't allowed to do. She'd been raised to shoot and act like a boy, though, so none of that bothered her.

That evening, they once again had supper with the Kings, but this time Sarah cooked for them all. "We'll always take turns," Sarah said. "There's no reason all of the burden should be on you."

"Cooking for my grandchildren will never be a burden!" Mrs. King said.

"I know. Just let me do my share so I don't feel like I'm taking advantage of your kindness."

Mrs. King had relented, but Sarah could tell she hadn't wanted to.

Sarah pictured the two King households being just on their own side of the property line, so she and Mrs. King could visit easily in the winter. They'd visit all year, but hopefully in the summer, they wouldn't be trudging through several feet of snow to do it.

Sarah made one of her favorite trail meals, which was cut up jerky, a gravy, and rice. Mr. King had glared at his plate, but after taking a bite, he'd nodded. "This is a fine supper, Sarah. I suppose I will let you cook for my grandchildren."

They all laughed at that, even Elmer. The two men had started talking again, and they were making plans to help each other with the building as soon as they arrived at Clover Creek.

After supper, Sarah and Elmer put the children to bed, and they went for their walk out onto the prairie. It had become something they did nightly, and Sarah was quite happy with their little tradition. Of course, she looked forward to the days they could simply make love in their bedroom once they'd reached Clover Creek, but for now, walks worked well.

While Sarah was spreading out their blanket on the ground, Elmer dug in his pocket for the present he'd made her. When she turned around, he took her hands in his and said, "Sarah, I love you. More than I thought possible. When I saw you in Independence, I admired your beauty. Now I admire your spirit and your love for others."

Sarah smiled. "I love you as well, Elmer. I don't know why you didn't approach me sooner, but I'm so glad you finally came to me. You are exactly what I needed after my father died, and I thank God for you every day."

He took the gift and put it in her hand, watching her face by the light of the half moon.

Sarah looked down at the object she held. It was a stick with a sharp end and carved into the other end was a rabbit. "This is beautiful! For my hair?" she asked, not wanting to use it for something other than its intended purpose.

He nodded. "I noticed you have been wearing your hair up a lot, with it being so hot, and I thought this might help you."

"Oh, it's wonderful." She threw her arms around him and hugged him close. "I can't believe you made this for me!"

"I'll probably make one for Poppy as well, but I wanted yours to be made first. Do you like it?" he asked.

"I absolutely adore it. I'll wear it proudly." Sarah looked up into his face and smiled. "Less than two weeks ago, I was certain my life was over. I didn't think I'd ever marry, and if I did, it would be to a man with a lot of children he needed help with. But you...you not only asked me to marry you, but you made my life so much better. The children love you. I love you. I don't know why I didn't take one look at you and know you were the man I was meant to marry."

"I don't either. I knew it the second I set eyes on you."

"Well, I certainly know now! You've made all of us love you with your quiet ways. I love your parents. I can't believe all of this came from me needing a driver."

He chuckled. "I needed a wagon as well. Don't forget that part of things."

"I don't think I could!" She took a deep breath. "We're going to all reach Clover Creek without dying, aren't we?" She still worried about everyone, but she could see they were so close to making it alive.

Elmer nodded. "I'll do everything in my power to make that happen, and I will do my very best by you for the rest of our lives."

Sarah smiled. "I know you will. You've already taught the children so much."

"My parents will teach them a great deal more," he said.

"I know. I'm so happy your parents just embraced all three of my siblings as grandchildren. The children are thrilled and so are your parents. It was like they were all waiting to meet one another. Sometimes, Poppy walks with your ma instead of walking with her friends."

"Ma told me. She's so happy that you suggested to her they were her grandchildren. Ma wanted a big family, but she was never able to get pregnant again after me. Having three ready-made grandchildren with the hope for more...It makes her the happiest woman on earth. Especially since we're all settling so close together."

Sarah rested her forehead on his shoulder. "I think that's perfect. I'll have the help I need with the children, and you have your father back."

"Did I ever thank you for making it easy for Pa and I to see eye-to-eye for the first time since I started apprenticing?"

"You don't have to thank me for anything. I'm learning so much from you about a better way to raise children. A way that makes the children feel loved and valued. I danced with both boys this weekend, and though they both acted as if they didn't want to, when we got out onto the dancefloor, they were pleased. My parents were the type of people who thought children should be seen and not heard. They would both say, 'Spare the rod and spoil the child' as if it was a battle cry."

"Did you get spanked often?" he asked, not realizing her parents had been so different from his own.

"Oh, yes. All the time. Father expected me to be the same with my younger siblings after Mother died, but I refused. I mean, I swatted their hands once or twice, but I never did more."

"Well, we're going to raise our children differently than either of our parents raised us. We won't be using the rod as often. And I won't tell any of them they have to go into a certain occupation simply because it's what I do. They'll have choices."

"That's all I ask." Sarah smiled. "I can't wait to have a child of our own. We need a little boy who wants to do nothing but build furniture."

He chuckled. "I would like that a lot, but I'm not going to force any of them to do as I want them to do. Besides, maybe we'll have all little girls who look just like their mother and learn to cook as well as she does."

"No, we need little boys to teach to be sweet, kind men. Knowing your mother will be able to help me with that makes it all sound easy." Sarah smiled. "We'll be in Clover Creek in just a few weeks, and we'll be choosing the spot for our home. Do you have any idea how excited I am to have my own home to organize and clean?"

"You like to clean?" he asked, surprised.

"It's not my favorite task in the world, but I will do it with a smile. Because I have a wonderful husband and three children I already love. And more soon. So many more."

"Just don't say that around my ma. She'll start asking you every day if you're expecting yet."

Sarah laughed. "She's already told me she wants at least a dozen grandchildren. I don't know if that's counting my siblings or not, but either way, I'll have as many children as God will give me."

Elmer smiled, tracing her cheek with his index finger. "And we're going to live happily ever after, right?"

"There's no other way we could live."

Ingram Content Group UK Ltd.
Milton Keynes UK
UKHW011530040723
424531UK00001B/84